The Hunt for Mr Jacks

The Hunt for Mr Jacks

Tom Wilson

ROBERT HALE · LONDON

Robert Hale Limited
Clerkenwell House
Clerkenwell Green
London EC1R 0HT

www.halebooks.com

2 4 6 8 10 9 7 5 3 1

Typeset in 11½/20pt New Century Schoolbook
Printed and bound in Great Britain by
Biddles Limited, King's Lynn

For my good friend of 40 years

John 'Goldfinger' Fleming

Nonpareil

CHAPTER ONE

Boris stood by a third-floor window of a house in Mayfair observing the outside world through a pair of slightly parted curtains. At 6.30 a.m. on a damp, misty London morning the square was more deserted than it would be later on. A solitary black car disappeared round a corner and, as it did so, a somewhat familiar sight appeared from round another but, where Boris had become used to the presence of bag ladies, it could still surprise him to see such a person walking the streets of one of the most affluent cities in the world.

This particular bag lady had first appeared three or four weeks back; since then she had become a part of the local scenery and Boris could not see her without being reminded of his dear old mother back in Bosnia. His mother too favoured wearing a red head scarf, and the too many coats, held round the middle with tied string, struck their own memory chords. How often had he seen his mother battle through the wind while being weighed down with a heavy load?

Boris's recollections were interrupted when Grigor opened the room door and asked if all was clear.

Boris said that it was.

'Then let's go,' Grigor invited. 'Our man is keen to get to his morning workout. We've guarded a few but this one has to stand as the vainest.'

'He wears Gucci to the gym,' Boris remarked, holding open his jacket to reveal the holstered pistol at his belt.

Grigor responded in kind, completing a ritual that served to tell each of them that the other man was armed and ready. 'Are we sure he's paying us enough?'

'Enough for now,' Boris responded. They walked along a landing and collected the man, who was wearing a designer suit and an impatient look. Grigor picked up the man's gym bag in his left hand, Boris positioned himself to the right of the man, then they escorted him downstairs and out of the building.

As Catharine turned a corner into the Mayfair square, she knew from that moment every move she made would be recorded by the plethora of CCTV cameras that hung from the sides of buildings, looking like long-guns focusing on their next target.

But Catharine was not at all concerned about her actions being recorded; her disguise was impenetrable. While researching the target's Bosnian bodyguards, she had uncovered a picture of the mother of one of them and it had inspired the costume she now wore. The weather-beaten old face, the red headscarf, the bulky coats and the apparently heavy bags had been wonderfully created by Leanna, but then Leanna could be a very creative girl. She might have failed as a ballerina but her way with costume and make-up had proved useful more than once.

As Catharine made her way slowly along the damp pavement, stopping as she always did to check the contents of a wastepaper bin, she considered yet again that things were not now as once they had been. For a month now she had been wandering in and out of this square, making herself a familiar sight to one and all. Four weeks of preparing for this morning and here she was only minutes from a triple kill and she felt not a flicker of excitement. She could get to missing the good old days with the KGB. At least then the targets were true enemies, the cause was just and, while the war with the West might have been cold on the surface, underneath it had raged like a furnace. All that went when Gorbachev dismantled the Berlin Wall. When the wall came down she found, like many of her comrades in the KGB, that her services were no longer required. In the real world, there were not many prospects for a female assassin and when Rasputin, a section chief with the GUR, informed her that he was forming an intelligence unit for the Red Mafia and invited her to come along, she jumped at the chance. Assassination was all she knew; what did it matter in whose name the killing was done?

In the beginning it was all so exciting. There were old enemies to be disposed of, power ladders to be climbed but, over the years of watching the power of the Mafia grow, her excitement in affairs had gradually diminished, corroded away by the boredom that was inevitable with repetition. It had been many years now since anyone had shot back at her and even longer since she had killed a target truly worth the killing.

This morning's target might be labelled a political dissident living under the protection of the British Government but he was, in fact, no more than a thief who had left his Mother Russia with the wrong people's money in his pocket.

And there are some people from whom it is very unwise to steal.

In her left gloved hand Catharine was grasping a bundle of carrier bags stuffed full of rags and newspapers. In her right gloved hand she grasped a solitary, bulging carrier bag that concealed a .40 calibre Glock 27 fitted with a sound suppressor.

Had her timing been too soon Catharine would have lingered by having a rummage in the next waste bin but, as it was, she needed to adjust her pace only slightly. Head down, mumbling to herself as bag ladies were wont to do, she watched as the target and his bodyguards came out of a house, down some steps to the street, turned and began walking towards her.

The target was easily identified by his bearing and expensive suit, and the way the bodyguards were positioned told her that they were not very professional. When she reached the three men they parted to let her go by. As she brushed by the target she flashed a set of rotten teeth and said, in a wonderfully dry cockney accent, 'Like the suit!'

The bodyguards were still chuckling when, three steps on, Catharine suddenly spun round, raised the carrier bag in her right hand and centre-shot each of them in the spine. As they fell, already dead, the target turned and stared at her, his face frozen by fear.

'A message from your old friend,' Catharine said in a soft voice. 'Thou shalt not steal from us.'

And then, as requested, she shot him in the face.

Mission accomplished, Catharine turned away and made off, her pace quickening with every step. Underneath the make-up and the bulky clothes, she was a fit, lithe woman and it did not take her long to turn a couple of corners and approach the grey Mercedes with the blacked-out windows parked by a kerbside.

A rear door of the Mercedes clicked open as Catharine drew near and she was quickly inside the vehicle and being driven off at a speed compatible with the laws of England.

'Was it a success?' Leanna asked as she guided the car through the growing morning traffic.

'The target and his bodyguards are down,' Catharine answered. She laid the carrier bags aside, then removed the headscarf and wig she had been wearing. 'But I wouldn't call it a success. I have become jaded. Even killing is not as moving as I remember it once was. Death no longer excites me.'

'I know something that will,' Leanna said, her young faced flushed as she looked at Catharine in the rear-view mirror. 'In fact,' she went on, her blue eyes wide with promise, 'I know lots of things that will.'

Fact was, even Leanna was not as exciting as once she had been but Catharine smiled. 'You must not be so forward,' she admonished. 'You know what happens to over-forward girls, Leanne. I shall be having words with you later. Do you understand?'

Leanna understood and smiled at the prospect.

CHAPTER TWO

Rasputin, as he was known, was a diehard Communist. When the Berlin Wall came down the Russian nation declared peace with the West but he did not; as far as he was concerned the Cold War never ended.

Rasputin hated what he thought of as the hypocrisy of democracy, a political philosophy much lauded merely because it had been created by the Ancient Greeks. What was rarely mentioned was the fact that their democracy applied only to Greek citizens; if you did not qualify then you were either an enemy of the state or a slave and he believed that America, with its concepts of democracy, practised the same hypocrisy. American democracy was there for Americans; after that, with the aid of its domestic henchmen such as Coca Cola and Big Mac and the insignia of the baseball cap, it was intent on enslaving the world. True, he was forced to admit, Communism had pursued the same intent, but then Communism gives to the people whereas Capitalism takes from them.

Fortunately for Rasputin his position as a section chief in the GRU meant that he was better informed than most, and he learned, two months in advance, that Gorbachev was going to open the gates to the West. His choice then had been either to join the newly forming FSB [Federal Security Bureau] or to branch out on his own. After but a moment's thought he decided to do the latter.

During those two months before the wall came down, Rasputin transferred funds to banks in Switzerland, Luxembourg and London. When he had funds enough he recruited similarly minded people, starting with his entire section and then going on to the military, the GRU and the KGB.

With the funds and the people acquired, Rasputin then approached a Moscow Mafia chief with whom he had already had dealings and, with a promise of power, talked him into their working together.

At the beginning there had been no organized Red Mafia as such, just a collection of different ethnic gangs who spent more time killing each other than they did fighting a common cause. With time, cunning and the necessary ruthlessness, Rasputin consolidated the Mafia, turning it into the respected criminal organization it had now become.

Unlike the Communists, this hybrid Mafia had learned that you did not have to wage war against a country in order to conquer it; you could conquer it from the inside merely by buying it. In the Capitalist world everything was for sale, it was simply a case of having enough funds and buying the right properties. The Americans originally bought Manhattan Island from the native Indians for a handful of beads. It would now cost much more to buy the island but, the fact was, Manhattan was for sale.

In moulding the Mafia into an updated version of the KGB, Rasputin created an army that had at least one barracks in every major metropolis in the world. The city streets had quickly fallen to his forces. In some, like Monaco and Marbella, they had been acquired by bribery and corruption, in Amsterdam it had meant an easily won war against the Turks and the Moroccans; Israel was being bought from the inside while, in America, his forces had only to contend with the Italian Mafia. Come the end, American gangsters were too family-orientated to be truly ruthless. Whereas the Sicilians and Italians never touched the family of an enemy, their Russian counterparts, in true KGB tradition, were capable of eradicating, an entire family from great-grandfather all the way down to the newest born.

It was an unpitying world in which, Rasputin believed, only the ruthless could triumph.

With his army busy conquering the streets of the democratic West, Rasputin then needed a weapon with which he could attack it from the outside. He found that weapon in al-Qaeda.

From its one-section beginnings, Rasputin's intelligence network grew until it was now on a par with that of the CIA. He had a chain of spies and informers that stood unrivalled. Some were his own people planted in power positions, some betrayed for profit while others were being blackmailed or coerced into supplying information. Between them, they kept up a steady flow of intelligence that was either used tactically or sold to interested parties.

A great deal of the intelligence that Rasputin gathered referred to terrorist activities. Reading one such report inspired him to a course of action. He, of course, knew of al-Qaeda's top people in Europe and he began his alliance by circuitously passing on information to them. With the third free sample he identified himself and eventually a meeting was arranged in Amsterdam. The meeting was attended by Omar bin Siff, the al-Qaeda chief who controlled al-Hashashin in Europe. Siff's name was very high on everyone's most wanted list, and by the end of the meeting a contract was agreed upon. For the annual sum of $25,000,000 Rasputin gave al-Qaeda sole rights to all anti-terrorist information gathered by the Red Mafia.

Fact was, Rasputin would gladly have given al-Qaeda such information for free but it was better that they believed that he was a mercenary criminal who worked for them for profit than have them know that he too was at war with the West and that it was, indeed, they who worked for him.

All those years of fighting the Cold War, all those guided missiles, all those nuclear warheads, yet neither America or Russia had ever fired a serious shot in anger. The two major world powers had fought second-hand wars in Korea and Vietnam but in the case of al-Qaeda, America had made an enemy of her own, one who was prepared to take the war to her. Al-Qaeda did more damage to America with four hijacked planes than the might of the Soviet Union had done over decades. It should have been Mig fighters that brought down the towers of capitalism but, come the end, what mattered was that they were razed to the ground.

At the conclusion of their first meeting, Rasputin and Siff shook hands. Neither had seen the other since. In these days of cyberspace there was no longer a need for dead-letter boxes. Information could now be transferred by e-mail to unknown locations hidden behind a wall of pornography. The need for personal contact was obsolete and, in such knowledge as he stood staring out over the canals of Amsterdam, Rasputin wondered again why Siff had requested a face-to-face meeting?

Omar bin Siff arrived exactly on time for his appointment. He was greeted respectfully but, even then, the Cossack, Rasputin's personal bodyguard, frisked him before escorting him upstairs.

When Rasputin shook hands with Siff he smiled inwardly at the difference between the man he had met in the past and the one he was now seeing. The beard had gone, the hair was fashioned Western style and the black robe had been replaced by a well-cut suit that came complete with crisp, white shirt and neatly knotted silk tie.

When the greetings were over the two men seated themselves, mint tea was served and conversation began with their discussing the latest American and British losses in Baghdad and Basra, their ongoing defeat in Afghanistan and Britain's reaction to the latest al-Qaeda threat to London.

As conversation continued, Rasputin was waiting for Siff to get to the reason for his being here. When, at last, Siff broached the subject, Rasputin voiced his surprise. 'I am surprised,' he said. 'I thought the contract on Mister Jacks was entirely a matter for those of your faith. Surely with a force like al-Hashashin at your command, you can hunt down and kill one man.'

'We are restricted,' Siff explained. 'We know that Mister Jacks is based in London and London is not a city around which we can move freely. Suspicion is in the air. An identifiable Muslim or even just a man with dark skin is watched by someone wherever he goes. And if we are not being observed by the public then we are being watched by security cameras. Did you know that there are more CCTV cameras in London than in any other city in the world?'

Rasputin nodded, 'I know,' he replied. 'But then the British survived the IRA, they were security conscious long before your people came along. I can appreciate your problem. You can't kill a man unless you first find him, and you can't find him if everyone is watching you.'

'That is difficult for us as Muslims,' Siff agreed. 'As Europeans, it should not prove as difficult for your people.'

'This is true,' Rasputin answered. 'The unofficial fatwa you have out on Mister Jacks comes with a rich reward for the one or ones who kill him ... all you would wish for, all you would will to be, does the reward still stand?'

'On oath of Allah,' Siff swore. 'Will you accept the contract?'

'I have a file on Mister Jacks,' Rasputin said by way of

reply. 'But nothing in depth; it is more a record of his exploits over the years. He's up there with the best. How many al-Hashashin did he take out in Europe? I heard eight, including the infamous Azrael, the one who liked making home movies. At the end Mister Jacks may prove difficult to kill, but the most difficult thing will be to find him. But I have faith in my organization, if we cannot find Mister Jacks then Mister Jacks is not there to be found.'

'You'll accept the contract?' Siff asked hopefully.

'I accept,' Rasputin responded. 'Even in the deadly world in which we live, Mister Jacks is a man who stands apart. He is a man who truly crosses scythes with the Grim Reaper. He tempts fate by carrying a small-calibre pistol that holds only five bullets. He is a man with a death wish and making his wish a reality will be my pleasure. But he is a man worthy of respect and I shall ascertain that he is killed respectfully. There shall be no covert poison for Mister Jacks, he shall die as he has lived and I already have someone in mind who I feel sure will be up to the task.'

'Excellent,' Siff commented with a rare smile as he and Rasputin sealed the contract with another handshake. 'Because Mister Jacks must die.'

'He will,' Rasputin promised.

*

When Siff left, Rasputin contacted Catharine in London and invited her to Amsterdam. He stressed that it would be a flying visit and that she should not bring any excess baggage along.

When he had made the call Rasputin gave thought as to how best to track down the elusive Mister Jacks. His knowledge of the man was somewhat limited. After himself, the only people guaranteed to know more were Jacob, a man whom Mister Jacks often worked for, and the CIA. The spymaster, Jacob, was a secret even to himself but the CIA promised to be a more positive source.

Although Mister Jacks had never directly worked for the Americans he had, by way of Jacob, more than once worked for them unknowingly. The Cassandra von Decker affair had initially been a CIA operation which they passed on to Jacob in the knowledge that he would pass it on to Mister Jacks. The CIA as good as treated Jacks as one of their own agents. They arranged for him to be backed up in Luxembourg, then broadcast his exploits on the Internet. If there was more to be learned about Mister Jacks then the old enemy, the CIA, were the people who knew.

As in the old days of the GUR, Rasputin had a man or two inside the Agency and he resolved to get in touch with them, with instructions to learn all they could about Mister Jacks.

When he had made his decisions Rasputin turned his

thoughts to the reward that would come with the death of Mister Jacks. The bounty was anything he might wish, anything he might will, and it was a promised reward backed up by the great wealth that ultimately supported al-Qaeda.

And, as it was terrorists who were making the offer, Rasputin thought with a thin smile, perhaps he would request that they bring down the Eiffel Tower, that nut-and-bolt monstrosity that for too long had been posing as art.

And, of course, there was always the Statue of Liberty.

When Siff returned to the al-Qaeda safe house in Amsterdam he contacted Saif al-Adel, one of al-Qaeda's warlords and chief of al-Hashashin and informed him that the Russian had taken up the contract on Mister Jacks.

'Good,' al-Adel responded. 'And are we certain he will use the one known as Catharine?'

'She is the best he has,' Siff answered. 'And as she is already in London—'

'You have located her?' al-Adel asked with evident surprise.

'We did not go looking for *her*,' Siff explained. 'We went looking for her companion, Leanna Korchov, the failed ballerina, and she was easily found. She has a mobile contract phone registered to a London address and when she is not giving her position away by phoning her mother and sisters in Krakow she is using a variety of credit cards in an attempt to buy up the West. I doubt very much if Catharine knows about the phone or the credit cards. She would not be so stupid as to allow them.'

'I agree,' al-Adel commented. 'The famous Catharine would be much too professional. The assassination she executed in Mayfair was a master class. I have had copies of the CCTV footage distributed to our training camps as a lesson on how to do it ... And *our* man, have you found him?'

'Yes,' Siff replied. 'But it was not easy, beginning with the need for him to be white. I was not exaggerating when I told Rasputin how difficult it was for an obvious Muslim to move about London and even more difficult for one to fly in and out of the country. I let my need be known to our people and three names were put forward. The same name was given by three contacts and I chose him. When I eventually tracked him down, I learned that he was on loan to the Taliban, fighting in Afghanistan as a sniper. When I spoke with Afghanistan, he was given an outstanding report. He has killed his share of foreign invaders and earned a reputation while doing so. He may have grown the beard, he wore the headgear and the garb, but his white hands identified him. The Taliban call him the Pale One but I have given him the codename Mithka, after the old Persian god of vengeance. He is sincere and idealistic. When I told him of his mission, his joy was there to see. He reveres Osama, to meet him is the only reward he seeks.'

'He sounds the perfect choice,' al-Adel judged. 'Where is he now?'

'In a safe house in north London,' Siff replied. 'The plan is that Rasputin finds Mister Jacks, then passes the location on to Catharine. When she moves Mithka moves with her. Catharine's flat in Elephant and Castle is already under surveillance. At the first opportunity the place will be bugged. It could work out that Mithka gets to Mister Jacks before Catharine does but, either way, Mister Jacks dies.'

'Does Mithka know about Catharine?' al-Adel asked.

'Not directly,' Siff replied. 'He has been warned that others are hunting down Mister Jacks but I did not want to diminish his role by telling him that he was merely the second gun. As things stand, we will have two first-class assassins out to kill the hated Mister Jacks. Surely one will succeed.'

'So long as he dies,' al-Adel stated. 'But it would be better for the reputation of al-Hashashin if Mithka was the one who actually killed him rather than if he was killed by a woman.'

'Even if she is of the manly sort,' Siff concluded with his second smile of the day.

CHAPTER THREE

Gabriella, the Marquise de Thionville, knew when she first met Billy Jacks that he was different from other men; in the twenty days and twenty nights she had spent with him since then she had learned just how different he was.

Billy was a labyrinth of contradictions constructed inside the paradox that was himself. So ruthless: so forgiving: so indifferent: so caring: so hard: so tender: so cold: so warm: the list went on and she had come to wonder if there was a beginning or an end to him, or was his capacity infinite?

More than once Gabriella had wondered just what kind of man she had fallen in love with. When first they met, he had been giving at least in the physical sense. Since then, it was as though each day he had taken back a part of himself, leaving him with less to give.

Physically, he had gradually regressed and, as there had not been much emotion there to begin with, without passion to drive him, he had become emotionally as far removed from her as he possibly could be. He had become so distant that she longed to see again the man to whom she had lost her heart.

Physically and emotionally Billy had switched off. These were secret withdrawals known only to herself, but where such coldness was not publicly betrayed, his condition was exposed in other ways. He no longer ate with the appetite she knew was his and when he laughed his laughter came from somewhere other than his heart.

Only yesterday, Ronald, her loyal butler, had remarked that judging by the half-eaten plates of food her guest was leaving, he appeared to have lost his appetite, that he was not as hungry now as he had been on arrival. Ronald was referring directly to Billy's appetite for food but Ronald was an astute man and she was certain he was alluding to much more than a half-eaten plate of boeuf stroganoff.

With the knowledge of him that she had gained, Gabriella was driven to surmise that the man she loved was enduring a hunger she could not feed, a hunger she could not name. She was expecting him to leave her any minute because if his hunger could not be fed at her table then he would need to dine at a table where it could.

She had best be prepared.

For the last couple of days, Billy Jacks's restlessness had increased until now he paced about like a caged panther who was missing the dangerous freedom of the jungle. It was always the same; every single time he found what he thought he had been looking for all his life, he ended up missing something from yesterday and needing more from tomorrow. A beautiful woman who loved him should be enough for any man but then, as he had learned, he was not *any* man and it was not enough for him.

It was time to be moving on.

Gabriella would know that such a move was imminent, but even so it was not going to be easy to tell her. How did he tell a woman who loved him that he was moving on merely in the hope of finding something different? But he would need to leave her now when he could still walk out through the door; if he held on much longer he would end up running away from her and he did not want her knowing just how anxious he was to be elsewhere.

Having made his decision he picked up his mobile phone and went downstairs to deliver the bad news to Gabriella. He found her in a sitting room, seated by a roaring fire, looking as beautiful as only she could look. He had barely greeted her when, as on so many occasions in the past, he was saved by the bell that rang courtesy of his mobile. When he answered the call by saying, 'Hello, Jacob,' hope was tolling the beat of his heart.

'Hello, Billy,' Jacob responded. 'Are you well?'

'That's not the word,' Jacks answered. 'But I'm hoping you're going to change my condition. What can I do for you?'

'You could do me a service,' Jacob responded.

On hearing those words Jacks became a man made lighter of heart. 'Just one?' he questioned with a smile manufactured by relief. 'Whatever it is, consider it done. When do you need me?'

'There's nothing to be done for a couple of days,' Jacob replied. 'If you could visit me tomorrow ... the Norwood house.'

'I'll be there,' Jacks said empathically. 'And looking forward to seeing you.'

'It's always a pleasure seeing you, Billy,' Jacob said, his words coated with a smile. 'And I have some news. Your friend with the little girl and the cat, whom you asked me to do a favour for, now resides in a nice house and a few days ago, she became a richer woman when she learned that she had won a quarter of a million on one of those prize draws that no one ever hears of anyone winning.'

'Nice one, Jacob,' said Jacks. 'How did Chloe take her change of fortune. I bet she just couldn't believe her luck.'

'She couldn't,' Jacob confirmed. 'But the lady I sent to take care of her convinced her otherwise. But I warn you, your friend suspects that somewhere you have a hand in things. She asked the lady if she knew anyone called Billy.'

Jacks chuckled. 'Chloe has a suspicious mind,' he said. 'But she'll never know for certain. When I see her next at her new house, I'll be playing the very surprised man.'

'Won't she wonder if you just turn up at her new address?'

'She's been wondering about me since I first bumped into her,' Jacks said, smiling again. 'But I know her mother's phone number, I'll get the address from her. I just hope dear Chloe can handle it all; she's a girl who finds life hard going.'

'My lady is advising her,' Jacob reminded him. 'And with you there in the background, I can't see your friend fall down.'

'I'll catch her if she does,' Jacks assured him. 'So, I'll see you tomorrow, Jacob. Probably around teatime, I'll ring you when I'm close and you can put the kettle on.'

'I'll be here, Billy,' Jacob promised.

'And I'll be there,' Jacks concluded.

Sitting opposite, Gabriella heard both sides of the conversation and though Billy had conducted himself as though alone in the room, her eyes had not left him for a second. In closely watching him, she witnessed a transformation that took her breath away. The somewhat deflated, hollow man with that hunted, haunted look in his eyes had magically become a man full of life, a condition that shone out of his now dancing eyes. Seeing Billy so transformed was as scary as it was wonderful. A few words from a man called Jacob was all it took and she wondered what spell he possessed that she did not. What was he offering that could so quickly turn Billy back into the man she had first loved, the man she would forever love. 'So you are leaving me? she asked, when at last Jacks turned his eyes on her.

'I could never leave you,' Jacks responded, looking at Gabriella as he had not done for a while. 'From here on, wherever I go you will be a part of me.'

'But not the major part?' Gabriella questioned.

'Major enough,' Jacks qualified. 'No one else ever fed me like you do. But, come the end, I suffer a different hunger.'

'The need for danger?' Gabriella asked.

'Danger is the bonus,' Jacks explained. 'What I hunger for first is the strange and new. A prison poet friend of mine said it for me when he wrote ...

> *It is not that the grass is greener,*
> *Or that hers is a sweeter kiss.*
> *But that the one I meet tomorrow,*

Is today the one I miss.
And the grass, though no greener,
Is a different grass than this.

'I didn't say he was a great poet, but he tells the story for me.'

How Gabriella smiled. 'You certainly have a way with you,' she granted. 'Anyone else might have reached for Byron or Keats but you reach for your friend the prison poet. Is he in prison now?'

'He's been in prison all his life.' Jacks answered. 'He's a prisoner of my mind. Every now and again he breaks out and I find myself left with a rhyme.'

'You wrote those lines?' Gabriella questioned.

Jacks shook his head. 'The poet inside me wrote them and sometimes he says it better than I can. But don't imagine me sitting starving by candlelight, quill in hand. When the verse comes, it comes complete, almost as though I am remembering it rather than creating it. But I gave up on verse when I couldn't find a word to rhyme with assassin. Besides, poets go hungry and as I am always hungry, I would quickly starve to death. I'm hungry now, perhaps you could order up a feast. I feel as though I haven't eaten for a while – but maybe that's because I haven't,' he concluded with an open smile.

Gabriella was none too pleased that someone else had

restored Billy's appetites but she was happy for him that he was once again the hungry man.

'It's never-ending with you, isn't it, Billy?' she queried. 'Every time I think I might have reached the top or bottom of you I find another layer waiting to be explored. You are the most intriguing of men. It is no wonder I love you. It will hurt me to see you go. I have a need of you.'

'You have a *want* of me,' Jacks corrected. 'I can only give you my word that I am not leaving for ever. Do you really think that I could live the rest of my life without at least once more hearing those wonderful, tantalizing sounds you make when we are as one.'

The look Jacks gave her, the image that formed in her mind combined to send a flush spreading across Gabriella's face. 'Look what you do to me,' she said with a suggestion of anger. 'I should be venting my wrath on you and here I am blushing like a girl. Has no one told you that I'm a *very* sophisticated woman?'

'I did hear something along those lines,' Jacks replied, smiling all over his face. 'But I dismissed it as a malicious rumour. You're just a woman, and a woman is all you'll ever need to be.'

'There, you have done it again,' Gabriella said accusingly. 'You can shift my heart at will. And as we are talking of women, can one ask who Chloe is?'

'You wouldn't be a woman if you didn't,' Jacks said, still smiling as he slipped into storytelling mode. 'There I was, crossing a wet, windy supermarket car park, when right in front of me a young mother with a little girl clutching one hand drops the shopping she has in the other. At that moment, it was as if the total despair of her life overwhelmed her and she burst into tears. As I approached, I heard the little girl ask if her mummy was all right and, in hearing the concern in her little voice, my heart was moved. I slipped into my rescue-a-maiden-in-distress guise and did just that.'

'I bet you charmed her,' Gabriella commented with a smile.

'It wasn't hard,' Jacks qualified as he remembered. 'Being as distressed as she was, she would have accepted a helping hand from Genghis Khan. As it was, I got her and the little girl out of the rain and home safely. Along the way the little girl told me her name was Jade, I told her mine was Billy, and we've been pals ever since. Jade's a wonder, she could charm the socks off a man. And it doesn't matter what you ask her, she always comes out with an answer. I can't recall why, but I asked her once if she knew what a genius was. "Of course I do," says she. "It's a man who comes out of a teapot like in Aladdin." Isn't that wonderful?'

Gabriella laughed. 'It is indeed,' she agreed. 'Einstein would have appreciated that one.'

'He'd have loved it,' Jacks said decidedly.

'You certainly get on well with the daughter,' Gabriella remarked. 'How well do you get on with the mother?'

'You're being a woman again,' Jacks pointed out with a grin. 'I get on very well with Chloe. At first she wouldn't let me give so I gave in Jade's name and, like all good mothers, she could not deny her daughter. Since then, they have become my family substitute. I treat the pair of them as my daughters, throw in a ginger tom called Rambo and I have it all. I pop in now and again, I get invited to Sunday dinner and go for walks with Jade and be young again for her. I'm already invited for Christmas and I'll be there. I've learned from being with Chloe and Jade that I'd never win any parent of the year competitions but I've also learned that I make a great Father Christmas. I draw the line at wearing the red suit but, aside from that, I'm well up for the part.'

'You see,' Gabriella declared. 'Another layer uncovered; there truly is no end to you. Do they never asked you what you do?'

'Chloe did once,' Jacks answered. 'I told her it was secret and she hasn't asked since. Like all kids, Jade doesn't care what I do so long as I keep bringing the presents. I like to give, it's my saving grace. Unless, of course, you think me beyond redemption.'

'You are certainly beyond,' Gabriella responded with a smile just for the man she loved. 'But I would redeem you without hesitation. You only have to call on me. And you will call on me, won't you, Billy? Can I ask when I might see you again?'

'So long as you bear in mind that tomorrow I may be dead,' Jacks replied. 'There's an army of assassins out to kill me but, allowing that I should live so long, I reckon early in the New Year.'

'One minute past midnight would be nice,' Gabriella said with an inviting look.

'I'll be doing my best,' Jacks promised, returning her look. 'My social calendar is looking good. Christmas with Chloe, Jade and a cat called Rambo, New Year with your delightful self, and before then I promised to visit Cassandra; all I need to do until then is keep breathing.'

'Cassandra?' Gabriella wanted to know. 'You've never even mentioned her name since you've been here.'

'Of course I haven't,' Jacks said. 'But that doesn't mean I haven't thought of her on occasions. Cassandra and I went through a lot together and when I get to seeing her, I'll begin by being curious to see how she has fared since Luxembourg.'

'And once you have satisfied your curiosity?' Gabriella wanted to know. 'Will you then seduce her?'

Jacks laughed. 'Actually, Gabriella,' he retorted with a quite wicked grin. 'I'm hoping that *she* is going to seduce me.'

As Jacks laughed again, Gabriella found herself laughing along with him. She did not exactly know what she was laughing at but the man sitting opposite could be so utterly disarming and it was better that she laughed along with him than started a war she would have no hope of ever winning. '*Je ne sais quoi,*' she said when the laughter subsided. 'That indescribable thing. The words were probably first voiced by a woman trying to describe a man like you ... If such a one ever existed. And she was probably as hopelessly in love as I am.'

'I wouldn't say it's that hopeless, Gabriella,' Jacks said. He leant closer and breathed her in. 'I don't have to leave until dawn. What do you say we first feast at the table and then I carry you upstairs and we feast again on the bed.'

Gabriella said she thought that a wonderful idea. Jacks was not the only one who was hungry; she had her own hungers to feed.

And she planned to sate herself.

*

From the start, Gabriella had known that the day would dawn when Billy Jacks would leave her but, even with her foresight, when that day did dawn and the man she loved departed with a kiss, a smile and a backward wave, he took with him the greater part of her heart.

CHAPTER FOUR

Rasputin was an old-fashioned prude who had never truly adjusted to the fact that Catharine was a lesbian. When she prepared for her trip to Amsterdam, she dressed in as feminine a manner as she could bear. She did not own a skirt or dress and eventually settled on a trouser suit that she had always considered a bit too frilly for her taste.

When Rasputin told her not to bring any excess baggage along he had been alluding to Leanna. If Catharine's butch presence offended him then Leanna's ultra-feminine submissiveness offended him even more. He had never met Leanna, never laid eyes on her, the very thought of her was offence enough. Back in Catharine's early days in the KGB, Rasputin had tried to seduce her. Since his discovering that she was a lesbian, she believed his dislike of Leanna and the other girls she'd had was based on the fact that they got what he did not. As things stood Rasputin would soon no longer need to concern himself about Leanna. Though the poor creature did not know it, their relationship was swiftly drawing to a close. The girl had lost that charming innocence. She had become too knowing, so wise that at times it was difficult to see who was dominating whom. Fresh blood was needed and, while in Amsterdam, she intended to look up some like-minded companions who would know of an innocent fern somewhere in desperate need of an older woman to instruct her in the ways of life.

That was the pleasure side of Amsterdam; the other side was causing Catharine more than a little concern. She rarely met Rasputin face to face and when she did the meeting usually involved a rebuke about her high-profile social life. She was afraid that he was going to render her redundant. It would not matter that she had successfully executed the Mayfair mission. The fact that she had been useful yesterday did not mean that she would be useful today. If Rasputin thought it was time for her to take up knitting then it was time she invested in some wool and needles.

On leaving the flat in Elephant and Castle, south London, Catharine scolded Leanna about her personal appearance,

THE HUNT FOR MR JACKS

instructed her to tidy the place up, patted her on a cheek, then drove to Heathrow airport.

From there, she flew club class to Amsterdam.

On arrival at Schipol airport she was met by a man holding up a placard bearing the name Velder. On identifying herself, she was led outside to a parked taxi, which the man used to drive her to Rasputin's headquarters in the city.

When she was delivered Rasputin kept her waiting. She had to endure the indignity of being intimately rubbed down by the Cossack, his personal bodyguard, before she was allowed entrance to his inner sanctum.

Rasputin greeted her with a handshake designed to crush a walnut and invited her to be seated. 'You did well in London,' he said as he took his place behind an ebony-wood desk. 'I have watched a copy of the CCTV footage and I appreciated the way you walked right through the middle of them.'

'It was the only way to do it,' Catharine explained. 'As ever, I would have preferred to use a long gun but, with such tight security on the square, there was just no way to set up such a hit. And besides, I had a message to deliver, I had to get up close.'

'How did he face death?'

'With fear and a very surprised look,' Catharine answered.

'The Mayfair bag lady!' Rasputin said drily. 'How many times is it now that you or your deeds have made headlines around the world? So many targets, so many years, I was thinking it might be time for you to retire.'

'I don't need to be young to pull a trigger,' Catharine said defensively. 'My eyesight's as good as it ever was, my hands are steady and I'm still the ruthless bitch I've always been.'

'I'm glad to hear this,' Rasputin said. 'Because, though I have been considering your retirement. I don't want you to go until I have put your talent to one more use. A rather special target has come up and it needs someone special to deal with him.'

Catharine's relief at not being made redundant fuelled her enthusiasm, it was there in her voice to be heard as she asked whether she knew this someone special.

'You know him by reputation,' Rasputin answered. 'And you know him as Mister Jacks.'

Catharine reacted with surprise. 'Mister Jacks?' she echoed. 'I thought his contract was restricted to al-Hashashin?'

'It was,' Rasputin agreed. 'But they can't find Mister Jacks and they've passed the contract on to me.'

Catharine pulled a face. 'They must have guessed that you'd give the job to me and it's not like them to use a woman.'

'They gave the contract to *me*,' Rasputin reminded her. 'You are merely my weapon and, when we get right down to it, you're man enough for anyone.'

'And more than enough for most,' Catharine retorted, turning an insult into praise.

'I must grant you that,' Rasputin said reluctantly. 'But how do you feel about killing Mister Jacks? I know how you respect him and his work.'

'Mister Jacks is very good,' Catharine agreed. 'And he was ruthless enough to backshoot Azrael: he blew him outside in. I can only respect him but, far from my respect being a reason *not* to kill him, it is my inspiration to do so. A man like Mister Jacks deserves to die at the hands of someone like me. Better I kill him than he gets run over by a London bus. Killing Mister Jacks will be my privilege.'

'You know the great price al-Qaeda has put on his head,' Rasputin said. 'Take down Mister Jacks and your reward will be great.'

Catharine worked exclusively for Rasputin but her ongoing contract allowed her one personal killing a year. In the business these are known as free shots. In the early days, with old enemies aplenty, she used her free shots regularly but it had been a long, long time since she had killed someone in the name of personal pleasure. 'I don't want any rewards other than the ones I claim for myself,' she stated.

'I want Mister Jacks to count as a free shot. I kill him because I want to kill him, I don't kill him for money.'

Rasputin was delighted with Catharine's response. He had hoped for enthusiasm but the fact that she was making it personal meant that she would now stalk Mister Jacks with a vengeance. 'As you wish,' he responded, as though her choice meant little if anything at all.

Catharine nodded. 'If I am to retire,' she said, her face much more animated than it had been when she arrived, 'then it would be good to do so after killing a man considered by many to be the best. My question has always been, is Mister Jacks truly ruthless or is he ruthless only from necessity? I know he can backshoot but it appears that he kills only those who are out to kill him. Could he walk up to a target in the park and shoot it in the face for no other reason than that he wanted to?'

'You had best hope you never learn the answer to your question,' Rasputin remarked sagely. 'Because, shortly after you do, there's a very good chance that you will be dead.'

Catharine smiled a most sincere smile. 'He would never get close enough to shoot *me* in the face,' she said, dismissing the notion. 'Even if I didn't know what he looked like I would see the threat coming. And I *don't* know what he looks like or where to find him. If al-Hashashin can't track down Mister Jacks are we sure we can?'

'As Europeans, my people can move around freely,' Rasputin pointed out. 'And I have resources that al-Hashashin can only wish for. Jacob is the man who knows most but I have tried more than once to penetrate his organization and I have found it impenetrable. After Jacob, the CIA knows most and, fortunately they are still fond of leaving the door to Langley open. I have a couple of men there learning all they can. Finding Mister Jacks is my task, yours is to kill him. I want you to return to London and await my call. Be ready to move at a moment's notice.'

'I will be,' Catharine vowed.

In the basement of a safe house in Muswell Hill, north London, two al-Qaeda intelligence agents were watching Catharine's London flat by means of intercepting a CCTV security system that had cameras covering the outside of the building, the inside, and the underground garage, which was shared by an adjacent office block.

The men watched Catharine leave for Heathrow and when, twenty minutes later, they saw Leanna Korchov leave on foot, they used a mobile phone to alert Sahid, their man on the ground.

Sahid was having a coffee in a café just round a corner from the target flat. When he received the call he responded immediately by pushing away his expensive cup of cappuccino and getting to his feet.

Sahid left the café looking like just another man in a suit carrying a briefcase but Sahid was not just another man. Sahid was al-Qaeda's best anti-security agent; he claimed to be able to open any lock, mechanical or digital, and then to circumvent any fitted alarm system. And, after eight years of faithful service, al-Qaeda had yet to fault his claim.

When Sahid reached the building he wanted, he turned into the underground car park. The car park was guarded by a tyre-shredder and a barrier that could be operated only by a coded remote that was issued to residents. But whereas these devices did a lot to stop the wrong car entering or a stolen car being driven away, they did nothing to hinder the comings and goings of a pedestrian.

The inevitable CCTV cameras were more interested in keeping an eye on the parked, expensive cars and Sahid easily stayed out of their field as he approached the door to a lift that led to the flats above. The lift was protected by a coded, push-button lock, but he had brought along his own smart remote and within seconds he was stepping into the lift, riding to the top floor.

The door to the flat was protected by the same style of lock as guarded the lift; it yielded its secret just as quickly and Sahid slipped inside Catharine's domain, the love-nest she shared with Leanna Korchov, known to one and all as the failed ballerina.

After taking a quick look around with his trained eyes, Sahid laid his briefcase on a table, opened it, then extracted all he would need to do the job he had been sent to do. The job took him eleven minutes but by then he had planted eight listening devices which between them were guaranteed to relay the spoken word from any room in the flat. He had been particularly careful when planting the two in the bedroom; in his experience the bedroom was where most truth was told.

His mission completed, after locking the doors behind him, Sahid left the building the same way as he had entered and returned to the café he had not long since left, where he ordered another expensive coffee and then rang the watchers to let them know they were tuned in.

The watchers had already seen Sahid emerge from the underground garage and, on receipt of his call, they contacted Siff to let him know that all was running to plan.

In an upstairs room of the Muswell Hill safe house, Mithka, the codenamed al-Hashashin assassin, lay on top of a bed, hands folded behind his head, reviewing a life that had led to him lying here waiting for a man to be found so that he might then kill him.

Mithka had been raised by a redneck family in Arkansas. He had been brought up to hate Jews, Blacks and Catholics but mostly he had been raised to hate America for the way it mistreated the people who had built the land in the first place.

Mithka's father was a Grand Dragon in the local branch of the Ku Klux Klan. Through them he led a subversive militia group who made their presence felt by blowing up power stations and firebombing federal buildings. His father's personal grievance against the government revolved around Forest Rangers, who thought they could tell him when and what to hunt, and tax collectors who wanted him to pay good money just for the privilege of living on land his grandparents had fought Indians to protect.

Mithka's father fought the fight but it was a fight he was fated to lose. One afternoon, two local policemen turned up at the farm with an arrest warrant, which his father refused to accept. A gunfight ensued during which his father's elder brother was killed and a policeman was wounded. After the encounter the whole wrath of the federal authorities descended on the farm and its occupants.

Even as a child, Mithka had been smarter than the average and, as he grew, his father decided that he should put his brains to use and become a lawyer, a position from where he could fight the enemy from the inside. The siege of

Stokey Farm happened when Mithka was studying law at an upstate university and he watched events unfold courtesy of CNN.

In a couple of days the farm and outbuildings were surrounded by an ever-increasing army of federal agents, FBI people, state troopers and heavily armed SWAT teams, their every move being recorded by invading satellite dishes, camcorders and reporters.

The inevitable shoot-out that followed culminated in the deaths of four FBI agents and three members of Mithka's family: his father, an uncle and his dear, sweet little sister, Emily Rose. The FBI accepted that they killed his father and uncle but they claimed Emily Rose had been caught in crossfire and that she had been killed by her own people. It mattered not to Mithka who fired the fatal shot, from his perspective the FBI had murdered the only person on the planet for whom he had ever felt genuine affection.

When he learned of the deaths in his family Mithka's already nurtured hatred of America blossomed into a cold fury that had yet to desert him.

Mithka knew the ineffectiveness of anti-American militia groups: lone bombers did little damage beyond the immediate and when he got to thinking how best he could make America pay for the murder of Emily Rose, he decided that he would join an army that was already at war with the USA.

America had been built on the war against the native Indians. That was quickly followed by a civil war; since then it seemed as though America was for ever at war with someone around the globe. At present they were at war in Iraq and Afghanistan. The problem in Iraq was that too many different factions were fighting America and each other and Mithka had no idea how to make an approach. But the people fighting the Americans in Afghanistan were a united force and he did know how to reach the Taliban, al-Qaeda's warriors in the field.

Mithka had read many times how al-Qaeda agents haunted Muslim colleges and universities, eager to recruit any dissident students into their ranks, and he decided to become one of those students, beginning by converting to the Muslim religion.

Faith was not needed, all Mithka had to do was memorize, imitate and remember to talk of Allah rather than God. He was a good student, who only three times let his hatred of his homeland boil to the surface. As he had calculated, three times was enough. Shortly after being accepted into the one true faith he was visited by a mullah from a local mosque and his pathway to revenge truly began there. He had been expecting someone to pay him a visit and it was easy for him to convince the mullah of his genuine hatred of his home-land and of his desire to fight against a government that thought little of killing innocent little girls.

The mullah proved to be only a go-between. A couple of days after they met Mithka was invited to meet a man representing al-Qaeda. When their respective positions were established Mithka told the man that he was prepared to kill Americans but that he was not prepared to do so by at the same time killing himself. He was a first-class shot, he was ruthless and felt sure a place could be found for him in the rank and file.

Mithka did not exaggerate about being a first-class shot. Like most Americans, he was born with a gun in his hand and, back home, his claimed ruthlessness was a proven fact. At the age of twelve he had gone on a hunting trip with his father, uncles and friends. The climax of the hunt came when his father brought down the mother deer with a neck shot, the anticlimax came when he brought down Bambi with a bullet between the eyes. Considering that the entire hunting party had bloodied their hands at sometime, to this day he could not understand their shocked reaction. Surely a deer, was a deer, was a deer?

Ten days after meeting the man from al-Qaeda, Mithka flew to Paris, France. He was contacted there and given the necessary papers, then he moved on to Lebanon where he found himself in one of those terrorist training camps of which he had so often read. He met no prejudice at the camp; the fact that he was white was not held against him, they were all warriors united by faith and by a shared hatred of America and all it stood for.

After three months' intensive training, a time when he learned all there was to know about high-tech weaponry, Mithka was honoured by being invited to join al-Hashashin, the world's killers supreme.

Mithka served al-Hashashin well; over the years, in their name, he killed many Americans: two CIA operatives in Beirut, a Jewish politician in Brussels, two advisers in Baghdad, the list seemed fated to go on for ever, but a couple of years back he had been loaned as a sniper to the Taliban fighting in Afghanistan and that was when he found his true purpose. Assassination had its place in the scheme of things, but to fight the enemy on a battlefield was a much worthier endeavour. The enemy shot back and it was much more pleasurable to kill a man who was ready to kill you.

Mithka grew the beard, he wore the robes, and even though he knew they called him the Pale One, he won the respect of the Taliban warriors. He would have been content to spend the rest of his life fighting beside such men but a few days previously he had been visited by an al-Hashashin agent, who told him to shave off his beard, to dress as a Westerner: he was needed for a special mission in London.

And here he was, lying atop a soft bed in a house in Muswell Hill. Was it only last week that he had been living wild in the mountains of East Afghanistan, laughing with bearded men, eating spicy food with his fingers?

Mithka had heard about the one known as Mister Jacks. His exploits across Europe, a time when he had killed eight members of al-Hashashin, had been the talk of the mountains, and while the Taliban talked of his death they also talked of him with the respect reserved for a fellow warrior.

Mithka learned there of the great price al-Qaeda had put on the head of Mister Jacks; he knew about the unofficial fatwa but he had never thought for a moment that he would be the man called upon to execute the mission. Being chosen for such a task was a great honour. When he had fulfilled the mission, when he had killed Mister Jacks, the name of the Pale One would echo around the mountains and all would speak it in reverence.

Osama himself would embrace him, his glory would be immortal.

CHAPTER FIVE

Billy Jacks enjoyed driving back to London from France, his thoughts shifting from the woman he had left behind and the man he was on his way to meet. Window down, wind about his face, the relatively open road before him, he savoured a sense of freedom he had not tasted for a while. For what seemed like ages he had been in the company of someone, now he welcomed back that assured solitude as a friend. People could be hard work, they were always looking for a response of one kind or another. He lived more easily with himself when there was no one else there, when he had nothing to respond to but his own thoughts.

On reaching London he drove to the garage in Catford, south London, where, taking his Ivor Johnson along, he exchanged the company Ford Focus for his Audi. While there, he recalled the night not so long ago when he had killed three men in the back room and Cassandra von Decker had wet herself at the top of the stairs. The fond memories he had! he thought with an ironic grin and then consoled himself with the knowledge that he was lucky still being alive enough to recall anything.

South London was a hive of memories, and as he journeyed to the Norwood house he felt almost at home, being on streets that were familiar. Gabriella's chateau with its forests and fields had its attractions but, after a while, all trees came to look similar and green fields had ever been foreign to him. There was nowhere quite like London, particularly on a wet, chilly December afternoon with the oncoming night slowly creeping up, swallowing the shadows as it came.

By the time Jacks reached the Norwood house he was a tired man, but a man most anxious to learn exactly what kind of favour Jacob needed doing. As he got out of the Audi the wind was blowing razor blades and he raised his coat collar, partly as a defence against the icy blast and partly to hide his face from the security cameras that dotted the outside of the house.

As ever, the doors unlocked as he approached then relocked behind him. When he entered Jacob's office he found him rummaging in a desk drawer. 'I want to see that hand come up empty, stranger,' he said in an American drawl, while pointing two fingers at him.

'That doesn't at all sound like John Wayne,' Jacob remarked with a smile as he exposed his empty, right hand.

'I should hope not,' Jacks answered as he and Jacob shook hands. 'It was supposed to be Clint Eastwood. How are you, Jacob?'

'Busy, Billy,' Jacob answered. 'The war against terrorism is an ongoing event. And you, Billy? How are you?'

'Once again, I had it all, Jacob,' Jacks replied as he took a seat. 'And, once again, having it all proved to be not enough. Sometimes I wonder about myself. You've got something you'd like me to do for you?'

'Not quite your usual but I'm hoping that you'll oblige me,' Jacob said. He extracted a photograph from an envelope and slid it face up across the desk. 'His name is Jonathan Durban-Sinclair, he's a private secretary to a cabinet minister and he's confessed to me to being a paedophile.'

Jacks stopped himself from picking up the photograph. 'I don't like paedophiles, Jacob,' he said in a cold voice. 'I'm not sure if I want to get involved in anything that has to do with abusing children.'

'Paedophiles don't like paedophiles, Billy,' Jacob commented. 'I can understand your obvious revulsion, but if you could be objective for a moment, I would ask you to hear me out. There's more.'

'I never could resist more,' Jacks conceded. 'Consider this is me being my most objective.'

'Seven months ago,' Jacob began, 'an associate introduced Sinclair to a child porn website. After three months of use, for which he paid the sum of five thousand euros, he was invited to a gathering. Sinclair took up the offer and on the appointed night, as instructed, he waited in the saloon bar of a pub in Bow until he was approached by a man who used the correct passwords. From the pub he was walked to a mini bus with blacked-out windows. On boarding, he found two other men wearing hoods. He was himself hooded and he and the other two men were driven out of London in an easterly direction. He believes the house he was eventually delivered to is somewhere in Essex. On arrival at the house, still hooded, he was guided inside the house. When his hood was removed he found himself in a luxurious bedroom, provided with a well-stocked bar. A curtain was drawn aside to expose a two-way mirror which revealed a collection of children. He was invited to make his choice ...'

Jacks raised a stopping hand. 'Do I want to hear any more, Jacob?' he asked in a tone that hinted at anger. 'I already feel like going out and killing someone responsible.'

'I won't spell it out,' Jacob said understandingly. 'Suffice it to say that three days after the event Sinclair was approached by two men. They showed him the photographs, told him about the film he had starred in and then told him what they would do if he did not do as they wanted.'

'They wanted him to become a spy,' Jacks concluded.

'Exactly,' Jacob concurred. 'Sinclair's position takes him all the way up to Cobra meetings. He was given four tiny listening devices, which he had to plant in the right places. The threat was that they would be tuning in the next day at noon and, if the microphones were not picking anything up they would immediately send a copy of the film to every MP in the House and, even worse, they would send a nice collection of photographs to his mother so that she could see what a pervert she had for a son.'

'So he went along with the blackmail?' Jacks asked.

'He did,' Jacob replied. 'But, the fact is, had it not been that his mother was terminally ill, he would have killed himself. Well, his mother died a few days ago and he came to me with a full confession. I have asked him to put off his suicide until after tomorrow. Part of the arrangement with the blackmailers is that at four p.m. on the thirteenth of each month he meets a man in a café in Stockwell. He gives the man five hundred pounds, the man verbally abuses him over a cup of tea and then they part until next month. Tomorrow is the thirteenth. I'd like you to keep the same four o'clock appointment and then see if you can learn who is behind it all. Such a sting as a website wasn't set up to entrap one man. I suspect others have fallen into the pit. Over the last year or so, too many anti-terrorist operations have led to nothing and I already suspected that there were leaks. You would be doing me a great service if you helped me plug those leaks.'

'You must have some idea who's behind the sting,' Jacks said.

'I believe I know,' Jacob responded. 'According to Sinclair, judging by the ill-fitting suits and accents, the man who delivered him to the Essex house and the one he meets in the café are Russian. This entire affair is reminiscent of the honey trap the KGB and GRU ran during the cold war. In those days, homosexuality or adultery was enough to cause ruin and disgrace; there's a logical progression in that the paedophile has become a target. The original honey trap concept was thought up by a man codenamed Rasputin. Back then he was a colonel in the GRU, the feared Military Intelligence Directorate; these days, he runs an intelligence unit for the Red Mafia and I suspect he's getting up to his old tricks.'

'The Russian Mafia?' Jacks questioned. 'What have they to do with military intelligence?'

'All their top people have a KGB, GRU or military background,' Jacob replied. 'The Mafia deals in anything where there is profit to be made ... people, drugs, guns, extortion, kidnapping, give it a name and they are in there somewhere. Intelligence is a highly saleable commodity, particularly if you don't care to whom it's sold. I suspect that Rasputin is selling anti-terrorist intelligence to al-Qaeda and I need to close the leaks before my department becomes obsolete. Will you help me, Billy?'

'Of course I will,' Jacks replied. 'I'd go a long way to injure al-Qaeda ... considering how far they're prepared to go to cause me an injury of the fatal kind. Any word on that front?'

'Not a whisper,' Jacob answered. 'But that's not to say you're not being discussed somewhere. Al-Qaeda have put a high price on your head.'

'Bring me the head of Mister Jacks,' Jacks said darkly. 'I'd best be careful then,' he went on, relaxing to a smile. 'Although I would find it difficult to be more careful than I already am. I figure I am safe enough. Only you and I know my location and I trust you with my life. I trust myself, so what do I have to worry about?'

Jacob could think of many things but he did not mention any of them. 'It's good to hear your confidence in me,' he said. 'I can assure you it is not misplaced.'

'I know it isn't,' Jacks agreed. 'Tell me where the

Stockwell café is and I'll be there tomorrow at four. I never know what you are going to ask as a favour. I imagine this, I imagine that, but I never thought to find you involving me with paedophiles, blackmail, spies and the Red Mafia – as if I didn't already have enemies enough.'

'You'll survive,' Jacob predicted. 'Surviving is what you do best.'

'There is that,' Jacks acknowledged. 'But there is one thing, Jacob. The way things now stand, I'm gonna need to sleep with a gun under my pillow and I won't be able to go to the corner shop without taking my Ivor Johnson with me. Can you arrange to make me legal? Get me a license or whatever is needed. I wouldn't want to get stopped at a road block or by a couple of curious Hecker & Koch carrying constables.'

'Of course, Billy,' Jacob agreed. 'It might perhaps be wise. I'll have you issued a Grade A security permit. In your real name?'

'I reckon,' Jacks replied. 'Then it'll match the name on my driving licence and insurance. It's a while since I've been William John Cranston, but being him can come in handy now and then.'

A little later the conversation drew to a close with a handshake, and a thoughtful Jacks set off for his flat in Lewisham, south London. Tired as he was, he was even hungrier and he took time out for a lamb rogan josh with boiled rice in a curry house he knew in Catford.

By the time he eventually reached his flat he was on the point of exhaustion, but he was not a man who let his physical condition dictate his actions and he showered before putting his Ivor Johnson under a pillow and sliding into his futon bed. He set his mental alarm clock for noon the next day and then surrendered to the tiredness that swept over him in a wave.

It had been a long, emotional month or so and, as the lady said, tomorrow was another day.

In the basement of a Russian mafia safe house in Golders Green, London, two members of a kidnap and extortion squad were sitting at a table that displayed a selection of computer screens showing different views of the Hampstead Heath house they were observing. They were watching courtesy of the house's external and interior security cameras. Such surveillance, together with the listening devices planted within the house, meant that they could hear and see the target whichever room he might be in.

At present the target, one Ivan Sek, was pacing an expensive carpet in a luxuriously furnished sitting room. He was wearing a black dressing-gown and a worried look to match. The watching men knew what was worrying Sek and, at a signal from one, the other rang Sek's mobile number. As the mobile rang they watched him on a centre screen as he hurried to retrieve it from an onyx coffee table, his anxiety apparent as he asked, 'Is that you, Jasmin?'

'I'm afraid not,' the caller replied in Russian. 'But I do know the whereabouts of your daughter. Should you want to see her again, then you must do exactly as I tell you. Do you understand?'

Sek understood only too well and, at the knowledge that his beloved Jasmin was in the hands of the mafia, his mouth dried with fear and his voice was hoarse as he replied that he did.

'Good,' the caller said encouragingly. 'It is best that you understand. The price of seeing your daughter again is a hundred million American dollars to be deposited in a bank nominated by us ... Are you agreeable?'

'I'll pay whatever you ask,' Sek swore. 'But please don't hurt my little girl.'

'We are businessmen, Mr Sek,' the caller responded. 'We do not hurt little girls but, should our arrangement prove unsuccessful, your darling daughter will be handed on to others who enjoy hurting the innocent. A quick course of heroin and before you know it, she'll be entertaining all kinds of sadistic perverts in some dark cellar in Moscow. I feel certain you would pay any price to prevent such from happening.'

As terrible, disturbing images flooded Sek's mind, he swore beseechingly that he would pay the ransom demanded.

'A wise decision,' the caller commented. 'We will contact you again tomorrow with instructions. In the meantime we shall be watching you. Any cry for help, any hint of the police and your little girl will pay a terrible price.'

'No police,' Sek promised. 'But let me speak with Jasmin.'

The caller chuckled. 'This is not Hollywood, Mr Sek. You are in no position to make demands. You will speak with your daughter when she's safe back home. We shall be contacting you as arranged.' He terminated the call.

'He'll pay,' the caller said as he watched Sek slump into an armchair, head on hands.

'They always do,' the second man observed.

CHAPTER SIX

As set, Jacks's mental alarm clock went off at noon; when it did he came instantly awake, his mind filling with the prospects of the coming day as he got out of bed, slipped on a black-towelling robe and went into the kitchen where he made a cup of strong, black coffee. He rarely ate first thing, hunger was something that caught up with him as the hours passed. On occasion he made himself a bowl of milky porridge but as there was no milk in the fridge, he easily talked himself out of eating anything.

Jacks carried his coffee back into the living-room cum bedsit, drew the curtains open and stood looking out over the dank, misty London landscape. In one direction stood a clutch of boarded-up tower blocks due for demolition, silhouetted against the overcast sky. In another direction were etched the outlines of giant cranes, which were busy erecting replacement buildings. As he took in the stark picture before him, he did not see it as one which might be used in a London tourist brochure.

When he had drunk his coffee, he went into the bathroom, did the necessary and then got under a hot shower, enjoying the water cascading around him as it brought his flesh to life. With paedophilia involved, he had a feeling that this was going to be a dirty mission and, as though in defence, he vigorously washed his hair three times.

Feeling wonderfully alive, Jacks got out of the shower, towelled himself dry, slipped back into his robe and returned to the kitchen where he made a second cup of strong coffee, which he drank while lying propped up on his futon.

When he felt ready, he prepared for the day ahead, beginning with laying out the clothes he would wear and collecting one or two things he thought he might need. When all was ready, he gathered his Ivor Johnson and then performed a ritual he always carried out after the completion of one mission and again the start of a new one. Because of his having spent three weeks in Europe this was the first time both rituals had been carried out simultaneously and as he broke the pistol down into its component parts, cleaning them and the sound suppressor, he did so with serious intent. When he had reassembled the weapon, he loaded it with five, copper-cased, explosive head .22 cartridges and then snapped them home with a flick of the wrist. Even though there was a spare belt of such bullets hidden in the boot of the Audi, just in case he needed more bullets and was separated from the car, he retrieved another belt of twelve from a secret drawer and laid it on the futon bed beside the clothes and the Ivor Johnson.

Better to have too many bullets than not have the one you need.

Suitably attired in a black reefer jacket worn over a grey polo-neck sweater, dark trousers and soft-soled boots, carrying a copy of the *Sun* newspaper, Jacks arrived at the Stockwell café at twenty minutes to four. With a glance at the huge wall-menu that seemed mandatory in such establishments, he ordered a large mug of coffee and a bacon sandwich.

As he waited for his coffee he took in the four workmen wearing donkey jackets and muddy boots who were sitting munching by one wall and the well-dressed old lady with iron-grey hair who sat mumbling to herself as she fiddled with a teaspoon. When his coffee was served, he paid the total bill and then carried the steaming mugful to a corner table from where he could view the whole café and the busy street outside.

When his order was delivered to him by a plump, ruddy-faced girl and a smile, he opened the *Sun*, took a bite of his sandwich then settled down to wait. As he munched the sandwich, he actually read sections of the newspaper. He learned little about what was going on in the world but he did glean a lot of useless information on the famous, of whom he had never actually heard. When he'd had enough of such nonsense he laid the rag aside while deciding that, entertaining as it was, it was a misnomer to call it a newspaper.

Sinclair arrived first. Jacks watched him as he approached the service counter and ordered a cup of tea. Sinclair had about him the look of a defeated man. The long, pale face with the hollow eyes, the slumped shoulders, the heavy gait each told its own tale of hopelessness but then, Jacks reminded himself, he was not only observing a self-confessed paedophile, he was looking at a man who had sentenced himself to death.

This was the first time Jacks had knowingly seen a paedophile and, as Sinclair carried his tea to a window table, he had to own that there was nothing there to give away the fact, not a hint of the perversity that lurked underneath. Sinclair looked like the man next door and that was probably who he was to someone.

The blackmailer arrived five minutes later. Whereas

Sinclair would never be recognized for what he was, the blackmailer had a somewhat shifty air about him. The ill-fitting grey suit, the carelessly knotted tie, the wide eyes, roaming here and there, brought to mind the Peter Lorre character in *Casablanca* while the swaggering gait coupled with a glimpse of a wrist tattoo caused Jacks to wonder whether the man had a past that included serving time in some prison or other.

As the blackmailer carried a mug of tea to the window table, Jacks took a mobile camera-phone from a pocket and brought it into play, ostensibly calling a number while actually filming the blackmailer as he seated himself across from Sinclair. At one point, the blackmailer looked around the café and, knowing he had captured him full face, Jacks terminated his supposed phone call.

As Jacks took a last sip of his now lukewarm coffee, he thought to himself that although along the way he had met his share of lowlifes, the two sitting by the window plumbed new depths.

The blackmailer who preys on the sins of the guilty and the paedophile who preys on the virtues of the innocent.

Judging his moment, abandoning the *Sun*, Jacks carried his empty mug and plate to the counter, thanked the plump girl in a broad cockney accent, then left the café, eyes front.

Jacks had seen the blackmailer cross the street outside and he did the same, loitering in a newsagent's shop doorway pretending to read a For Sale/For Rent noticeboard as he kept an eye on the café. His Audi was parked a street away but even if it proved impossible to follow the blackmailer on wheels, he would at least be able to follow him on foot to wherever he was parked. All he needed was the blackmailer's car number; with that and a full-face photograph Jacob's people would have enough to unlock all his secrets.

Sinclair left the café first. As Jacks watched him disappear round a corner he wondered whether the paedophile would kill himself, as he had threatened, and if he did, what method would he use? He did not see Sinclair as a man brave enough to kill himself violently, if he did commit suicide he would probably choose a drug overdose, perhaps the same drug as had been administered to his fatally ill mother.

A few minutes later, the blackmailer left the café, crossed the road and walked past Jacks. Jacks mentally counted to five, then fell in behind him, following him as he weaved his way through oncoming pedestrians, several of whom were loaded down with Christmas shopping.

The blackmailer turned right and led Jacks up the street where his Audi was parked. There were plenty of parking places on the street so, by the time the blackmailer crossed into another side street, Jacks had figured that he had come to the café on foot, a deduction that was proved correct when the man he was following suddenly turned into the pathway of a house up ahead. Jacks identified the house by the lamppost on the pavement and by the tree next door, crossed the street and then walked past it, observing as he went.

The house was semi-detached with the other side not only empty but boarded up. The curtains were closed upstairs and down and paint was peeling off the front door. A street number was not discernible so Jacks checked the next two houses then did a backward count. A signpost gave him the name of the street and a postcode, so, when Jacks eventually returned to the Audi, the first part of the job was done.

With a photograph, his address and postcode, Jacob would not only be able to uncover the blackmailer's secrets, he would be able to uncover the secrets of his ancestors.

Jacks sat in the warmth of the Audi for a few minutes thinking about what he was getting himself into. If this was a paid job he would probably resign on the spot. But this had nothing to do with material gain; he was doing a favour for Jacob, a man who had befriended him before they had even met.

A few years back, when he had still been known as Billy Cranston, an assassin known as Creel had been hunting him down. At the time he thought his friend, Solomon Fox, was the man who supplied the information that helped him to outwit and eventually kill Creel, but he learned later that the information was second hand and that it originated with a man known as Jacob.

After the Creel incident, at Jacob's invitation they met. During the course of conversation Jacob asked if he could do him a service. That was how the relationship started and ever since he had been doing favours for Jacob while Jacob in turn did favours for him. It was a close relationship based on the understanding that each had for the other.

Other than himself, Jacob was the only male friend Jacks had.

Jacob lived in a dangerous world, it was a place that Jacks usually liked to visit, but not this time; this time Jacob's world was coated in slime. Jacks had only seen the blackmailer and the paedophile across a café floor but already he had an unclean feeling about him.

When Jacks felt entirely ready for committal, he called Jacob on his mobile, passed on the photographs and the information gathered, then settled down to pass even more time by just waiting.

Half an hour or so later, Jacob returned the call. 'The blackmailer's name is Gregory Volochivich,' he began. 'Known best in the Moscow underworld as the Snake. Thirty-four years old. Born in Moscow to a prostitute, GRU informant mother who went on to run the mafia's brothels in the city. She still does. Inevitably perhaps, he grew up to be a pimp and procurer. At seventeen he was sent to prison for mutilating a girl by throwing acid in her face, at twenty-six he was given four years for sexually assaulting a nine-year-old girl, at present he is wanted by Moscow in connection with the kidnap of a four-year-old girl. A most unsavoury character.'

'I can think of another word,' Jacks said icily. 'And the house?'

'Owned by a housing association that supposedly finds homes for Russian émigrés,' Jacob replied. 'Read that as the mafia securing safe houses in London. I already have people looking into the case. What's your next step?'

'It's just gone six,' Jacks said with a glance at his watch. 'I'll give it a couple of hours or so to let the neighbourhood settle down for the night and then I'll pay our man a visit. I'll learn from him all he knows, then I'll pay you one. I don't like this one, Jacob,' he continued in a sombre tone. 'This one's dark, I can't see any laughs along the way. But, I'll see it through. After all, am I not a man of my word?'

'You are indeed,' Jacob confirmed. 'I can only say that I appreciate your endeavour.'

'That's good to know,' Jacks responded drily, then terminated the call.

With yet more time to kill, Jacks secured the Audi and walked back to the newsagent's across the way from the café, where he purchased a copy of *The Times* and a cheap biro pen.

From there, he found a pub that sold food, ordered cottage pie and an American dry ginger, paid the bill, then tucked himself away in a corner from where he had a clear view of the entrance.

With most citizens at home for tea, the bar was empty but for a rather obese man standing at the far end of the counter who had just drained a pint glass. As he took in the scene Jacks reflected on the vastly different lives each of them led. If the obese man thought anything at all, he probably thought the man in the corner doing *The Times* crossword had just finished another hard day at the office, when in fact the man in the corner was thinking of how best he could extract information from a man who was certain to be reluctant to part with it.

The cottage pie was delivered and Jacks whiled away the time eating and filling in *The Times* crossword. By the time he left the pub he had cleared his plate and finished the crossword. Now he was a man who knew what needed to be done and was prepared to do it.

Jacks was very good at doing what needed to be done.

Very good indeed.

CHAPTER SEVEN

In order to avoid passing the front of the target house, Jacks made his approach by walking a circuitous route and coming in at the far end of the street. The cold, damp, misty night was keeping everyone indoors and all was quiet as he reached the lamppost and turned left on to the pathway that led up the side of the house. The downstairs curtains were still drawn but a flickering light in a top corner window suggested that someone was inside watching TV and he designated it as the target room.

Guided by the faint light from the lamppost, Jacks moved silently up the side of the house, avoiding open rubbish bags displaying empty beer cans and vodka bottles. He trod carefully and stopped when he reached the end of the wall, checking the rear area for any sign of light. Seeing none, he slipped round the corner, avoiding more rubbish bags as he did so, and approached the back door which he found secured by the original, old-fashioned Yale lock. He dealt with that easily and slipped into a kitchen, closing the door behind him, leaning back against it, letting his eyes adjust to the darkness in the room as he fitted a silencer to his Ivor Johnson.

A door to the right of a sink loaded with unwashed table-ware let a strip of light pass underneath it. As his eyes adjusted to the dimness so did his ears attune to noise. Beyond the loud, humming fridge, he heard what he at first thought was the miaows of a kitten but, as he neared the inner door, he realized that he was in fact hearing the plain-tive sobs of a little girl in distress.

In response to the sounds an angry Jacks, Ivor Johnson at the ready, turned the handle of the inner door and pushed it wide open to expose a world of perversion and despair. Seated on a facing couch, a man wearing a dressing-gown was watching child pornography on a TV screen. As Jacks stepped up and stuck the Ivor Johnson in the man's face, on the TV screen, he caught a glimpse of a little girl's tearstained, pain-distorted face. As he heard her sob-broken voice plead over and over that she wanted her mummy, inside him something died. 'Switch it off. Switch it off ...' he said over and over again, trying to block out the heartrending cries coming from the TV. 'Switch it off. Switch it off,' he went on until the fearful-faced man found the remote and pressed the right button. When silence descended Jacks, using the Ivor Johnson, sideswiped the man across the face. As his left cheek split open, the man squealed, and Jacks sideswiped him again, splitting open his right cheek.

Jacks's rage was such that he could easily have beaten the man to death; it was only the fact that he needed information coupled with his remarkable self-control that prevented him from doing so. With great effort of will he took a couple of backward steps and stood pointing the Ivor Johnson at the cowering man's now bloody face. Staring at him with a loathing that, until now, he had not known he possessed, breathing slowly, he fought the power of his blind rage, bringing it under control until it evolved into a cold fury that felt as strange to him as his loathing. When he knew he could trust his voice, he said, 'Sit on the floor. Back to the couch. That's it,' he encouraged as the man obeyed. 'Now stretch your arms out along the couch and spread your legs as far apart as you can get them ... Wider,' he instructed, kicking the man on an ankle. 'That's it,' he concluded, satisfied that the spread-eagled man sat defenceless at his feet. 'Move wrong and you are a dead man.'

'Who are you and what do you want?' the frightened man asked through blood-streaked lips and a terrible Russian accent.

'I'm the avenging angel,' Jacks replied, his eyes black. 'And what I want, Gregory Volochivich, better known as the Snake, is information. This afternoon you met a man called Sinclair. I want to know all about the blackmail and all about the people running the show.'

'They'd kill me,' the Snake pleaded.

'I'm sure they would,' Jacks agreed coldly. 'I can see my problem here,' he went on, holding the Snake with a look that spoke of death. 'Although you're afraid of me, you are still more afraid of the mafia. I need to make it so that it's me you fear first.'

A soiled handkerchief was lying on the couch. Jacks told the Snake to pick it up and then stuff it in his mouth, encouraging him with a kick to a leg. 'What I'm going to do next,' he continued as a confused Snake did as he was told, 'is going to hurt, and I don't want your scream to disturb the neighbours.'

So saying, Jacks leaned forward, gripped the Snake's right wrist in his left hand, pulled the arm straight, stuck the silenced Ivor Johnson into the elbow joint, bent the arm up and pulled the trigger.

The explosive-head bullet left the barrel travelling faster than the speed of sound. When it hit bone, it shattered the Snake's elbow joint into a hundred splinters that shredded his flesh on their way out. The resulting, shocking pain sent the Snake's head snapping back, his tear-filling eyes almost popped out of their sockets, sweat erupted on his pale brow while his muffled scream came out as an extended whine.

'I told you it would hurt,' Jacks said in a tone preserved in ice. 'The question is, are you now more afraid of me? Will you tell me all you know, or shall I do the same to your other elbow?'

As the Snake urgently nodded his head, wet eyes wide with fear, Jacks knew that the man at his mercy was ready to divulge any secret even if it began by his needing to betray his mother. 'Wise,' Jacks whispered. 'Take that rag out of your mouth and get ready for confession. Bear in mind that I already know most of the answers, lie to me once and you sacrifice your right elbow.'

With a trembling hand, the Snake obeyed the instruction. 'You're going to kill me, aren't you?' he questioned in a pain-racked voice.

'I'm not a killer,' Jacks lied. 'I'm here for information. Tell me all I need to know and you live. Let's start with Sinclair. How many people are you collecting from?'

'Six,' the Snake replied unhesitatingly.

'Six?' Jacks questioned, prodding the Snake's injured arm with a gloved finger. 'I was told more than that.'

'I swear I only deal with six,' the Snake gasped as he was

hit with a fresh burst of pain. 'I think there are more collectors but I don't know.'

'I believe you,' Jacks said. 'Next question. Where's the evidence?'

'That table,' the Snake replied, indicating with a nod of his head.

'The drawer?' Jacks questioned as he approached it.

'There's a switch just above it,' the Snake told him, each word riddled with agony. 'Press it and the top lifts on hinges.'

Jacks pressed the switch, lifting the table top to reveal half a dozen sealed, padded envelopes, each bearing a name. He recognized Sinclair's name, another name he knew and was a little surprised to read a woman's name on another. How naïve of him to think that only the male of the species abused little children. A dozen or so DVDs in cases took up the rest of the space, one title read *Julia Comes to Play*, another read *Susanne Learns a Lesson* and that was enough for Jacks as yet again he had to rein in his fury.

'Right,' he said in a voice he barely recognized as his own. He took two cans of beer out of a carrier bag, dumped them and replaced them with the padded envelopes. 'Just a few more questions, then I call the police. They'll get your arm fixed up and they'll protect you from the mafia. Who can say but with what you know, you might be able to cut a deal. Where were these films made?' he concluded, holding up the carrier bag.

With hope of life and freedom from pain as incentives the Snake was now eager to please. 'Rosewood House in Essex,' he replied, going on to give Jacks the exact location.

'This next question really matters,' Jacks continued as he hunkered down between the Snake's outstretched legs and pointed the Ivor Johnson at his face. 'How many children are in the house?'

'I haven't been there for a while,' the Snake replied. 'They come and go. Four, six, maybe eight. I've never known more than that.'

The images forming in Jacks's mind sickened him. 'And where do these children come from?'

'Mostly East European orphanages,' the Snake replied, as though telling how he bought a washing machine cheap in a sale. 'Shop around, and you can buy them by the dozen.'

Inwardly, Jacks flinched. 'You said mostly,' he pointed out. 'Where do the others come from?'

'Kidnappings,' the Snake replied. 'Some mothers sell their kids. I can give lots of information to the police. I know enough to hang a lot of people.'

'I bet you do,' Jacks agreed disdainfully. 'Only two more questions and I make the call.' He rose to his feet, towering over the Snake who cringed beneath him. 'How regularly do you keep in touch with the people you work for?'

'They contact me about once a week,' the Snake replied. 'And I heard from them yesterday.'

'That'll give you time before they miss you,' Jacks said encouragingly. 'Last question. Do you know a man called Rasputin?'

'The Chief?' the Snake questioned. 'I know of him but I don't know him. Nobody knows Rasputin. Now, can I get a doctor, I'm in agony.'

Not for much longer, Jacks thought as he took a backward step. 'I'm trying to find the word for you but I'm failing miserably,' he said. 'Perhaps paedophile says enough. By any name, I am going to kill you.'

'But you said you'd let me live,' the Snake pleaded.

'If I did, then I was lying,' Jacks confessed. He lowered his Ivor Johnson and shot the Snake in the groin; then, as the Snake's body straightened like a conjuror's wand and his mouth opened wide, he raised his pistol and shot him between the eyes, silencing the coming scream before it could be heard.

From there, carrier bag in his left hand, Ivor Johnson inside his jacket, Jacks left the scene like a man fleeing a plague-infested city. The damp evening had turned into a wet, rainy night and as he walked quickly, he held his face up to the sky, letting the icy droplets cleanse him as they refreshed him.

Jacks felt sick. When he reached the Audi, he left the door open, put one foot on the pavement and surrendered to his stomach's demands by throwing up into the gutter, watching as the rain flow washed away the cottage pie he had eaten earlier.

Jacks retched for a good few minutes. When his stomach had sacrificed enough, he closed the car door, wiped his face with a handy tissue then sat there watching raindrop tears slide down the windscreen as his mind was haunted by the image of the little girl's tear-stained face and he heard again her pitiful cries.

Without doubt, this was the darkest night of his life.

And it was not yet over, Jacks thought as he switched on the engine and set off for the house in Norwood. He had done the favour for Jacob. What was in the carrier bag and what they would inevitably lead to would enable him to plug all the leaks. He had kept his word, the contract had been honoured, from now on he had his own cause to serve.

A certain hatred had been born inside Jacks and, being as he was, he could do no less than pursue its terrible demands.

And pursue them he would.

With vengeance.

CHAPTER EIGHT

The minute Jacks walked into the room, Jacob knew he was seeing a man different from the one he had seen earlier; the aggressive body language, the black eyes set in a stone face told their own story. As they shook hands he said. 'You don't look yourself, Billy. Are you all right?'

'I'm a highly disturbed man, Jacob,' Jacks replied. He emptied the six padded envelopes out of the carrier bag on to the desk top. 'There should be enough in these to plug all your leaks,' he said coldly before going on to give Jacob the location of Rosewood House. 'And that's it for now,' he went on. 'Before we discuss anything, I need a shower, I feel as though I've been contaminated by evil.'

'That bad?' Jacob questioned with concern.

'Worse,' Jacks stressed. 'Tonight I saw a little girl's face on a TV screen. I heard her cry for her mother and I'm afraid that the image is going to haunt me for the rest of my life. I need a shower, Jacob.'

'Of course, Billy,' Jacob directed Jacks to a bathroom down the hall. 'You'll find everything you might need in there.'

'What I need is oblivion,' Jacks said. 'For now, learn all you can about Rosewood House but don't make any moves until we talk. I have something to tell you.'

'And I have something in particular to tell you,' Jacob responded.

Jacks nodded in acceptance. 'And perhaps you could arrange for a gallon of black coffee.'

'Anything to eat?'

Jacks shook his head. 'The way I feel, I don't care if I never eat again.'

When Jacks departed for his much needed shower, he left behind a concerned Jacob; if Jacks had lost his appetite, he could only wonder what else he might have lost.

And that look in his eyes.

Jacks got under the shower with the hopes and expectations of a man stepping into the river Jordan. On other occasions he had imagined that he carried with him the smell of death; tonight he was carrying a different odour.

He had been in the same room as corrupt depravity, and the stench of evil lingered still.

When he had washed his body Jacks then slowly turned the temperature of the water down until it flowed icy cold before turning it up as hot as he could bear. He repeated the process three times, finishing with a cold blast. When at last he emerged from the refreshing cascade, he felt revitalized in body, but where soap and water had washed away the stench of evil it had not washed away the terrible dark images that persisted in invading his mind.

There was not a detergent made that could wash *them* whiter than white.

When Jacks rejoined Jacob, he found a mug of strong, black coffee waiting. A couple of sips of the dark brew and his mouth again tasted human. 'Me first,' he began, sitting down opposite Jacob. 'When I walked in on the Snake, he was sitting on a couch watching child pornography. I hurt him a little and would no doubt have killed him there and then but for my being there to do a service for you. At first he was reluctant to impart information so I shot him in the right elbow. After that he divulged all. I encouraged him with a lie about handing him over to the police and then, when he had told me all I wanted to know, I killed him. I shot him first in the groin, then I put one in his head ...'

Jacks paused a moment to take a couple of mouthfuls of coffee while Jacob waited in silence.

'The groin shot is for the police to read when they eventually get there,' Jacks continued. 'With all the evidence around the place, I reckon they will read it as a revenge attack on a paedophile, either personal or one carried out by a vigilante. The elbow shot might confuse them a little but, come the end, particularly after they learn the Snake's past, I don't think they'll care much either way. As we agreed earlier, nobody likes paedophiles.'

'I don't know what to say, Billy,' Jacob owned with a slow shake of his head. 'On other occasions I have heard at second hand, or read in the papers about the acts you committed in my name. This is the first time I have come face to face with one of the … executants. I won't attempt to justify your killing such a creature; you will find your own justification, but I will sincerely apologize for the obvious distress I have caused you.'

'You weren't to know what I'd walk into,' Jacks said. 'I just hope it all was worth it. Was it?'

'From my position,' Jacob answered, 'I could not have wished for more. The contents of the six envelopes will bring about at least a cabinet reshuffle. By tomorrow morning all these leaks will be plugged and who knows what else there is to be learned along the way. I know one of the blackmail victims personally.'

'I thought I knew a name,' Jacks came back, giving Jacob a sharp look. 'And now I know all the names, I want to read about their downfall in the press. Assuming Sinclair kills himself, I want the other five to go down hard. I know how fond the security services are of making deals. I'd hate to think someone might make a deal with a paedophile.'

'No deals, Billy,' Jacob responded. 'You have my guarantee on that. Come the dawn they will all be under arrest with each of them facing a long term of imprisonment.'

'And Rosewood House?' Jacks asked. 'What's the plan there?'

'A dawn raid,' Jacob replied. 'I've already been in touch with the Essex constabulary. They're on stand-by. Special Branch are preparing and I'm gathering my own people. We'll move in at first light.'

'Sounds good,' Jacks conceded. 'But I have a plan of my own. There's a good chance that there are kids in Rosewood House, and I shudder to think what might happen to them between now and daylight. When I leave here I'm going to the house to see what I can do about the place. It's gone midnight, so let's say I get there for two, half past, take some time to check it out, make an approach and I'm in by three. If you don't hear from me before dawn, go ahead with plan A. If you do hear, then send in the troops as soon as. I've done the favour for you, Jacob, from now on I'm doing this for myself and I'll be wearing the colours of a little girl with a tear-stained face.'

Jacob almost smiled. 'I would not have presumed to ask so much of you,' he said. 'But as you are ready to do as much, I shall encourage your endeavour. When you were showering I located Rosewood House on a route-planner and I printed out a copy. This may prove useful,' he concluded, sliding the print-out across the desk top.

It was Jacks's turn to almost smile. 'You know your man, Jacob,' he said as he folded the map and put it in a pocket. 'No doubt about that. Now that I've told you what I had to tell, it's your turn with the news.'

'A certain coincidence has emerged since last we spoke, a coincidence with not a little irony,' Jacob began. 'I have a man inside the CIA—'

'Who doesn't?' Jacks interjected.

'Who indeed?' Jacob agreed. 'And this man informs me that Rasputin is trying to find Mister Jacks. It seems that the Red Mafia has taken up the contract al-Qaeda have out on you. It appears that whereas Rasputin is coming at you from one end, unbeknown to him you are coming at him from the other.'

Jacks chuckled darkly. 'I certainly have a way of making enemies,' he observed. 'Al-Qaeda, al-Hashashin and now the Russian mafia. Perhaps I should try a different brand of soap!'

Jacob smiled to hear that Jacks had not entirely lost his sense of humour; he had once said that if he ever did, he would be a man as good as dead.

'You can trust your CIA man?' Jacks asked.

'Trust?' Jacob questioned. 'The man's a double agent and only a fool would trust a man who betrays one side or the other. Trust is not an issue but his information has always proved reliable. If Rasputin has taken up the al-Qaeda contract then there is only one assassin he would send after you ... You will know of Catharine, a woman with quite a reputation.'

'The creator of the double-shot?' Jacks questioned. 'I've heard of her all right.'

'And you'll have picked up on the Mayfair bag lady story?'

'One and the same?' Jacks asked.

'Almost certainly,' Jacob confirmed. 'I am having her tracked down. She herself would be difficult to find but I have heard already from my people that her girlfriend, Leanna Korchov, the famous failed ballerina, is leaving a trail of credit card purchases across London; believe it or not, she actually paid her mobile phone bill with a card. Their whereabouts will soon be known. Catharine is much too professional to condone such irresponsible behaviour; it would seem that she is paying for her proclivity for pretty, brainless girls.'

'I didn't know Catharine was a lesbian,' Jacks remarked with a grin hovering. 'I'll never live it down if I get taken out by a dyke. So I'd best make sure I outlive her. Judging by the Mayfair hit, she's very good. I didn't know she worked up close. But then, the security around the square's tight. I counted eight cameras in one photograph I saw in the press. Must have made it difficult to set up a long shot. Catharine's good, al-Hashashin are good but it doesn't really matter how many people are out to kill me. Whoever they are, they first have to find me. And as you and I are the only people who know where I am, then, as I said before, what do I have to worry about?'

As before, Jacob could think of many things but he did not mention one. Instead, he quoted Polonius. 'This above all things, to thine own self be true,' he said with feeling. 'Profound words I first read a long time ago. I grew up fully intending to honour the advice but, bit by bit, in the name of position or ambition, I betrayed the greater part of me. Most of us do. It's a built-in part of our survival mechanisms. But not you, Billy, you found another way to survive, one that has let you stay true to yourself. You have never betrayed yourself and for this alone, I hold you in great respect.'

'I appreciate the thought,' Jacks responded. 'But, the fact is, Jacob, I could never betray the way I am because the way I am is all there is.'

Jacob smiled.

*

It was coming up to half past midnight when Jacks left Jacob, with a parting handshake. Before driving off for Rosewood House, he opened the Audi boot and retrieved a pair of light-intensifying binoculars and reloaded his Ivor Johnson. After disposing of the Snake, he had only two bullets left in the chamber and he was hoping to run into more than that number of targets.

The more the deadlier.

CHAPTER NINE

Rosewood House sat on the edge of Waltham Forest close to the town of Chigwell and though Jacks knew roughly where he was heading, the printed route map got him there by the quickest way. This was no night for going the long way round or for getting lost in the wilds of Essex; this was a night when he truly needed to get where he was going.

The route to Rosewood House involved driving all the way through south London and then all the way through the East End. According to the print-out, the journey should take fifty-one minutes but Jacks could not imagine a period, day or night, when such a journey would take such a short time. Whoever had worked out the time scale must have been travelling at seventy miles an hour and never met a traffic hold-up or a set of lights along the way. It was on its way to one o'clock in the morning but London is a city that never closes down for the night and he still ran into the odd hold-up, his patience growing thinner with each one he met. He drove into a particularly bad delay on the east side of the Rotherhithe Tunnel. By the time he got free of it, his sense of urgency had mushroomed into a terrible worry that was haunting his mind.

If there were children being held captive at Rosewood House, then right at this moment something terrible could be happening to one of them or to all of them. The terrible images that sprang unbidden into his thoughts caused him to consider the policemen and women who hunted down paedophiles as a full time occupation. He himself had only caught a glimpse of the abuse inflicted on children but the police saw such practice in all its detail over and over again. However did they live with such first-hand knowledge when the little he had seen looked set to haunt him for the rest of his life? It was little wonder that so many police officers turned to alcohol as a comfort or chose suicide as the only way to escape their nightmares. Such men and women had his sympathy. With his back-street upbringing, Jacks had grown up with a certain mistrust of the forces of law and order, but he had to own that they were the first line of defence in the face of evil. Without the police, without the laws they upheld, overnight one half of the country would murder the other half.

A cynical observation perhaps, but Jacks had no doubt as to its veracity.

When Jacks reached the suburb of Forest Gate, he turned left and followed a signpost for Chigwell, a route that took him along the fringes of Waltham Forest. His route continued with a left turn at a war memorial, which would lead him directly to the front door of Rosewood House but, as he did not want to arrive at the front door, he drove past and took the next left turn. According to the map, the road looped round the rear of the house and he smiled coldly into the darkness when it came into view to his left, sitting in a dip.

Jacks parked the Audi off road behind a clump of trees, then, binoculars in hand, he found a spot on the other side of the road from where he could best observe the house. As he focused on the only lighted window that he could see, the moon, which had shone full all the way, disappeared behind a bank of cloud. As more clouds gathered the stars went out one by one and he was left standing in a darkness that was never seen in a city. An icy wind picked up and he was struck by the foolish thought that it was going to snow.

Jacks had good night vision and, as his eyes adjusted to the gloom, he refocused on the side of the house below. With it now being shrouded in total darkness, any glimmer of light was visible. As well as the curtained window, another to the top right showed a fainter light, which he thought was being generated by a lamp.

Three vehicles were parked in a courtyard lit by a solitary lightbulb: a dark minibus and two cars. Jacks figured the minibus was the one that had transported Sinclair and the other hooded paedophiles and he hoped that it had not delivered a similar cargo earlier. The very thought of breaking in on paedophiles at play had his mind turning away in loathing.

Please God the minibus was only parked there. If this was the case, the two cars suggested the presence of a maximum of eight people, a minimum of two. Jacks found himself hoping there were more rather than fewer.

Wanting to look round the house and using the light-intensifying binoculars to plot a path, treading carefully, Jacks made his way down a slope and into some trees. The icy wind had picked up speed and as it howled and screeched, making the bare tree-branches creak and groan, he never gave a thought to having his position betrayed by a snapping twig; given the noise around him, he could have driven up in a tank.

Jacks moved in a circle. When he eventually came out of the trees he was directly facing the back of the house. He had checked thoroughly and it looked as though neither security cameras or alarm boxes protected the house. Not that he cared if the place was belled to the skies. He would reach a point when he would need to wake up the house; if it worked out that the occupants woke sooner than planned, then that was all right with him. After all, he was not a burglar out for some loot, he was a killer out for some bodies.

As he made his way round the house a reflected square of light on the lawn disappeared, telling Jacks that at least one person was in the upstairs room. As the patch of light vanished, the silver moon popped out from behind a bank of clouds and Jacks saw this as his signal to move.

The binoculars had served their purpose and Jacks laid them aside at the base of a tree before drawing his silenced Ivor Johnson. Guided by moonlight, the icy wind ripping at his face, he ran to the back of the house, stood a moment in anticipation of outcry, then continued to work his way slowly round the house, looking for the best way in. He was checking out a suitable window when his eyes were drawn to a faint strip of light at the base of the house wall.

Figuring that the light came from a cellar, Jacks got down for a look. All he could discern through the dirty strip of glass was a black ceiling seen through the top of a line of steel bars. The light was on, the bars told their own story and, as his mind yet again painted unwanted pictures, he made the cellar room his first target.

Urged by the terrible mental images that persisted in invading his mind, Jacks chose the first window along and quickly dealt with the old fashioned latch-lock. The window squeaked as it opened and he climbed into the house like a man who had been climbing in and out of windows all his life, stepping wide on entry just in case there was a trembler alarm hidden underneath the corridor carpet. The corridor had windows along one side, doors along the other. Guided by faint moonlight, he made for the door revealing a strip of light, smiling for the moon when he saw a key so thoughtfully left for him hanging on a hook.

Jacks reasoned than anyone careful enough to lock the cellar door would first have been careful enough to switch off the lights behind him. From this he deduced that someone was locked in the cellar. Jacks knew about being locked in a cellar and when he unlocked the door to expose a steep flight of steps going downwards, he came face to face with a deep-rooted phobia he had lived with since early childhood.

He closed the door quietly behind him and, with Ivor Johnson pointing the way, Jacks tentatively made his way downwards while memories from his past crashed in his head, his heart thumping in his chest as the terrible memories united then multiplied into an army of ghosts.

Exercising willpower in the face of phobia, Jacks descended the steps then turned right into a large space that was nothing like the cellar of his memories. His cellar had been damp, musty, grey and running with giant spiders, this cellar was decked out like a medieval torture chamber. The rack, the stocks, the iron maiden, chains, ropes and hooks, they were all there and, as his mind was flooded with other, unwanted terrible imaginings, Jacks fervently hoped that this was a room where only adults came down to play.

The cellar contained an inner room and Jacks again appreciated the fact that a key hung ready on a hook. Ivor Johnson at the ready, holding his breath in dread of what he might see, he unlocked the door and then caught it again when he saw a young, blond-haired girl, dressed in jeans and coloured top lying on a bed asleep under her coat. The girl stirred as he approached and, as her big brown eyes opened wide, he held a finger to his lips, then whispered: 'Don't be afraid. I'm here to help you.'

In response the little girl sat up, clamping a hand over her mouth to stop herself from making a sound.

The cellar might have stirred unwanted memories but Jacks knew that above all other considerations it was a ready-made trap and his first instinct was to escape from it. 'Slip your coat on,' he whispered. When the little girl had done so, he took her by her right hand, whispered, 'Trust me,' then with Ivor Johnson pointing the way once more, he led her out of there, being somewhat embarrassed as they passed through the torture chamber, wondering what she must make of it all.

Jacks was relieved to get out of that cellar. When he reached the corridor, the still silent little girl holding tightly to his hand, he opened the first door he came to. Seeing it empty but for a large couch lit by the moonlight that streamed in he led her in and closed the door behind them.

'There you go,' he said softly. He hunkered down so as to look the little girl in the face, positioning her so that her back was to the door, which he could watch over her left shoulder. 'That's step one,' he continued. 'Can I know your name?'

'I'm Jasmin Sek,' the little girl whispered back. 'And I've been kidnapped. Did my dad send you to get me?'

Jacks shook his head. 'No,' he replied. 'I'm here on another rescue mission. I found you by chance and I'm very happy that I did. Do you know who kidnapped you? Did they do it for ransom money?'

'A man and a women took me after my hockey match,' Jasmin whispered in a grown-up manner. 'And of course it's for ransom money. Why else would they kidnap me?'

Jacks did not tell her. 'Of course,' he whispered back.

'Sometimes I can be so stupid. Your dad will be missing you. The sooner I can get you back to him the better.'

'You'll take me home to my dad? Jasmin asked excitedly, clamping a hand over her mouth as at the end her voice rose.

'You have my word on that,' Jacks vowed.

But Jacks's word was not quite good enough for Jasmin. 'Do you promise?' she whispered.

'I promise,' Jacks whispered back.

'Cross your heart?'

'Cross my heart,' Jacks responded and did just that. 'But, before we leave, there is something I need to do. Have you any idea how many adults are in the house?'

'I only saw the ugly woman who brought me my meals,' Jasmin answered. 'She pinched my arm last night because I didn't eat all the supper she'd cooked for me.'

Oh, did she, Jacks thought.

'But she's not the same woman who kidnapped me,' Jasmin continued. 'I heard voices sometimes on the outside and lots of cars coming and going … oh, and a man laughing.'

'You don't miss much, do you?' Jacks responded with a small smile. 'And children?' he asked. 'Have you seen or heard any children?'

'I haven't heard any,' Jasmin replied. 'But I did see two

little girls when they brought me here. I think they were going to a party?'

'Why would you think that?' Jacks enquired.

'They were wearing party frocks and ribbons,' Jasmin whispered.'

Inwardly, Jacks flinched. 'You're a very observant girl,' he said. 'And a very brave one. I'm going to ask you to be brave a little while longer and I need a promise from *you*. Where I'm going next, I can't take you along and I want you to get behind that couch and to stay there until I return. Will you give me your promise as I gave you mine?'

Jasmin smiled a little moonlit smile. 'I promise,' she said.

'Cross your heart?' Jacks asked as she had asked of him.

'Cross my heart,' Jasmin responded as she did just that, looking at him, her brown eyes wide with trustfulness.

'Bless you,' Jacks said, and his heart melted like chocolate on a hot stove. 'Bless your little heart.' He squeezed her hand as he made sure that she was securely ensconced behind the couch.

'I'll be back,' he said, and then set off to do what he had come here to do.

It was time to wake up Rosewood House.

CHAPTER TEN

On leaving Jasmin, Jacks turned left and followed a corridor that led eventually to the house's main reception hall, which he found lit by moonbeams streaming in from a high window. He had no difficulty in reading the scene.

The obligatory grand staircase led up to a central landing with a balcony each side. The front door was to his right, an ornate table standing in the centre of the hall boasted a tall copper vase displaying a clutch of dead reeds. As he took it all in he assessed his position.

When Jacks moved he did so as a man cognizant of a future that he was about to make happen. Treading softly, he walked to the front door, unlatched it, then opened it as wide as it would go, giving entrance to the still howling wind which brought a flurry of fine snowflakes along for the ride.

From there he walked quickly back, side-kicked the ornate table and was in the position he had assigned himself almost before the copper vase hit the stone floor. When it did, it bounced and bounced, clanging and clanging, the noise echoing and re-echoing round the hollow hallway. He thought that the clamour would have been enough to awaken Lazarus.

Above, Jacks heard two doors being opened. A male voice shouted something in Russian, a second male voice called something back in the same language, a light came on and footsteps hurried across the landing and down the stairs.

From the shadows Jacks watched two men as they came into view. One was barefoot, wearing a grubby vest over a pair of trousers, the other was similarly unshod and wearing a pair of striped pyjamas. Each was carrying what looked like a 9 mm Stechkin in his right hand. When they reached the bottom of the stairs their urgency diminished when they felt the wind blow about them, saw the open door and the copper vase still rolling about on the floor. They read the set-up as it was intended to be read and lowered their guns. Pyjamaman said something in Russian, then walked towards the open door leaving Vestman to pick up the rolling vase.

On other similar occasions, Jacks had given warning to the targets as to what was coming, but this time he did not waste his breath on such niceties. For other targets he had held a certain warrior respect but he held no such respect for paedophiles or for kidnappers of little girls.

Choosing his moment, Jacks stepped out of the shadows, raised the silenced Ivor Johnson and shot the kneeling Vestman in the back of the head. Then he turned the pistol on the unwitting Pyjamaman and shot him in the same place, sending him smashing bloody face first into the door he had just struggled to close.

From there Jacks bounded up the stairs. He had just reached the top when a woman in a nightdress, struggling to get into a dressing-gown, came sideways out of a door along the facing corridor. Fast as you like, he did a right swerve then stood with his back to the balcony wall, arm raised, Ivor Johnson held ready.

The dark-haired woman in the checked dressing-gown hurried past Jacks, calling the name Georgi as she reached the balcony railings, then leant over for a look. As she reacted on seeing the bodies below, Jacks stepped up behind her and stuck his Ivor Johnson in the back of her scrawny neck. 'Do you want to die?' he asked softly. 'No? Then I suggest you tell me what I want to know … I was told that there was more than three adults in the house. Where is everyone?'

'You missed them by a couple of hours,' the fear-filled woman replied in an atrocious Russian accent. 'They've all gone to the Wimbledon house.'

'Where exactly in Wimbledon?' Jacks asked with an encouraging prod from Ivor Johnson, turning his face away as he smelt her rank body odour.

The woman recited the name of a house and its address.

'And now,' Jacks insisted, 'take me to the children. And don't turn round, I don't want to see your face.'

'I've never harmed them,' the woman whined as she turned away, the gun still held to her head and led the way down a corridor. 'I'm like a mother to them … I take care of them.'

'I'm sure you do,' Jacks agreed icily. 'How many children are there?' He followed the woman up a short flight of stairs and along a door-lined corridor, switching on the lights as he went.

'Four.'

'Four?' Jacks emphasized the question with a prod from Ivor Johnson. 'I was told more.'

'There were eight,' the woman hurriedly answered. 'But they took four to Wimbledon.' She led Jacks along what appeared to be a dead-end corridor, bypassing a couple of doors until she stopped, pressed a discreet wall stud and the end wall slid open to reveal a flight of carpeted stairs that led up to a bright-blue door.

'The key?' Jacks asked.

'It's not locked,' the woman replied.

'What's in there?' Jacks indicated a door to his left.

'Nothing,' the woman answered. 'An old roll of carpet, I think.'

'Lead on,' Jacks instructed, prodding her again.

The woman led Jacks into a bare moonlit room. When she was far enough inside and he had closed the door behind them, he told her to stop, pressed the pistol into the back of her head and said, 'Give me one good reason not to kill you.'

'I'm a woman, I'm unarmed and I swear I've never touched the children,' the woman pleaded in a terror-filled voice while the rancid smell of her fear wafted from her in waves.

'That's three reasons,' Jacks said as he smelt her terror. 'But none of them is good enough. In the first place, you're not a woman, you're a child abuser, in the second, I don't care that you are utterly defenceless and in the third, when you say you never touched the children, did that exclude doing this?' He raised his left hand and cruelly pinched the woman's upper left arm. 'From the little girl in the cellar you forgot to mention,' he concluded. Then, as the woman squealed, her head snapping back in reaction to the sudden, sharp pain, he pulled the trigger, blowing her face all over the room while sending her hurtling to the floor, where she lay spread-eagled, lifeless as a scarecrow.

Looking down at the obnoxious specimen whom he had just executed, Jacks stood a moment, controlling his breathing, calming his raging heart, steeling himself for what he had to do next. There were four abused children in an attic room who needed rescuing. The very thought of having to face them aroused in him a certain apprehension. The children were certain to hold a deep mistrust of adults. How would they react if a strange man was suddenly to walk in on them?

Would they cry?

Would they scream?

With such thoughts, Jacks removed the three empty cartridges from the Ivor Johnson and replaced them with live rounds. He was pretty certain he had dealt with all the adults inside Rosewood House but he would hate to run into more opposition and find himself short of a bullet, particularly when he had a pocketful.

Rearmed, Jacks left the room, closed the door and then went to find what he thought could be the answer to his dilemma over the children. He had an ally under the roof. If the children saw him with Jasmin, a girl who trusted him, then perhaps they would look on him with friendlier eyes.

On his way back to Jasmin Jacks stopped long enough to

collect the two dropped Stechkins and to drag the two bodies into an anteroom and out of sight. He would need to walk Jasmin round the bloodstains but, as far as he could, he would shield her from the reality of what he had done during his absence from her. It was not just that he did not want Jasmin seeing the dead bodies, he did not want her to know that it had been he who had made them dead.

It was turning out to be a time for making unusual allies; earlier Jacks had called upon the wind for its assistance and here he was on his way to ask as much from a little girl.

He just never knew with life.

CHAPTER ELEVEN

Jacks found Jasmin behind the couch, arms wrapped around her, looking as though she had not moved an inch since he had left her. 'You *really* are a brave girl,' he said as he offered her a helping hand. She accepted it and he pulled her to her feet.

'My dad says that I'm a *very* brave girl,' Jasmin amended. 'Will you take me back to him now like you promised?'

'I keep my promises,' Jacks stated, hunkered down, looking Jasmin in the eyes. 'But before I take you home I need your help.'

'My help?' Jasmin questioned in surprise.

'Your help,' Jacks repeated, then went on to tell her about the four children being held prisoner in the attic. 'They're the children I came here in hope of rescuing,' he explained. 'But I'm afraid that if they just see me I might frighten them. I reckon I won't frighten them if they see me with you. Maybe they'll see me as an adult they can trust.'

'Have they been kidnapped?' Jasmin asked.

Jacks said that they had.

'And their dads wouldn't pay the ransom?'

'It's a different kind of kidnap,' Jacks answered, almost at a loss for words. 'But they still need rescuing. Will you help me? I'm supposed to be tough, but underneath I'm just a scaredy cat.'

Jasmin smiled an understanding smile. 'Of course I'll help you,' she said. 'But they won't bite you, you know.'

Sad as he was, Jacks could only smile back. 'Thanks,' he said sincerely. He took her right hand in his left and they left the room side by side.

Moonlight had deserted the hallway; it was dimly lit but even so Jacks suspected that Jasmin had seen the blood-stains when she asked, 'Where are all the bad people? Did you shoot them? I saw your gun before.'

'No, I didn't shoot them,' Jacks lied. 'I took them prisoner then locked them in a room. The police will find them when they get here.'

'Do you still have your gun?' Jasmin enquired.

'Yes,' Jacks replied, afraid she was going to ask to smell

the barrel to check whether it had been recently fired. 'It's in my coat pocket.'

'That's cool,' Jasmin said decisively, once again leaving Jacks somewhat at a loss for words.

As they made their way up to the attic Jacks switched on the lights that he had missed first time round. When they reached the bottom of the stairs behind the hidden panel, they stopped for a moment. 'Here we go.' Jacks sighed as he gave Jasmin's hand a squeeze.

'I'll go first if you like,' Jasmin volunteered.

The sincere offer touched Jacks to the heart. 'I appreciate the offer,' he said softly. 'But I'm not *that* big a scaredy cat. We'll do it together.'

So saying, tightly holding hands, Jacks and Jasmin climbed the stairs. When they reached the brightly painted door Jacks did not hesitate, opening it quickly to reveal a dimly lit room, the shapes of eight beds with children asleep in four of them while the four that lay empty each told its own terrible story.

Reaching round, Jacks found a light switch. When he clicked it down, three central pink-shaded lights came on and the gloomy room was instantly transformed into one of vibrant colour. The scene, with the pastel-coloured walls and ceiling, the Disney characters painted behind fairy-tale beds, the rocking-horse, the teddies and soft toys, the slippers, the folded dressing-gowns laid over the brightly coloured duvets, under which four children lay fast asleep, might seem to reflect an image of happiness, comfort and love. His knowledge of the reality, of the terrible deception being perpetrated, greatly disturbed his sensibilities. As his insides shifted, something inside him was unlocked, and for a moment he thought he was going to burst out crying. Such a flood of emotion was unknown in his experience and it took a great effort of will to hold the tears at bay.

The lights, the movement, disturbed a little boy who quickly sat up straight in bed while giving Jacks the most disturbing, accusing look.

'It's all right, kid,' Jacks said in soft assurance. 'I'm not here to hurt you.'

'He's a nice man,' Jasmin said in support. 'He's already rescued me. Now he's going to rescue you.'

The sound of voices woke the other three children one by one until Jacks found himself faced by two little boys and two little girls, all sitting up straight in bed, each looking at him with frightened eyes. For Jacks, it was a quite chilling moment but as he recognized a little girl as the one he had seen briefly on the screen back at the Snake's house, his heart went out to her on the wings of a smile. 'Was it something I said?' he asked foolishly as he sat down on the edge of the little girl's bed, inwardly flinching as she instinctively pulled away from him. 'I really am here to help you,' he went on, in a tone desperate to convince. 'I'm here to help all of you. I promise I'll see you all safe.'

'You can trust him,' Jasmin said supportively. 'Honest you can.'

Jasmin's 'Honest' finally convinced the children as, one by one, they got out of bed and Jacks found himself in an arc of innocence, four children wearing teddy-bear pyjamas and hesitant little smiles. For Jacks that was a most touching moment but he was quickly coming to see his gathering emotions as a threat in that they could easily distract him from the job at hand. He knew the attic room was as much of a trap as the cellar had been and his first instinct was to get out of there, for if he did not feel safe enough, how then could the children? 'I don't like it in here,' he said truthfully. 'Does anyone know a better room, one with a switch-on fire?'

After discussion and much nodding of heads, the children agreed that the best room was the big one downstairs with the fake log fire. 'Right,' Jacks said. 'Slip on your dressing-gowns and slippers. We're getting out of here.'

The children obeyed with an unnatural alacrity that disturbed Jacks. When they were ready, they stood in a line, hands by their sides as though awaiting inspection. The picture before him tore another pang of Jacks's heart and, once again, he was brought close to tears. To cover his discomfiture, he knelt down beside the little girl from the video and asked, 'What's *your* name?'

'Anna,' the little girl replied shyly.

'Right, Anna,' Jacks responded, his heart melting all over again, 'You and I will lead the way and Jasmin will be with your friends,' he went on in a shaky voice, taking Anna's right hand in his left. 'Are you ready?'

'I'm ready,' Anna replied in a little voice.

'Then let's go,' said Jacks.

Leading the children from that attic room was the finest moment Jacks had ever lived; he was flushed with a sense of accomplishment beyond any he had ever experienced.

For a moment, he thought his heart would burst.

Freed from the confines of their Disney prison, the children opened up a bit, chattering among themselves as they wondered about what was next going to happen to them next. Holding tightly to Jacks's hand, Anna negotiated the smaller attic steps successfully but as they reached the main staircase it quickly became apparent that the steps were just too big for her little legs and, with no hesitation whatsoever, Jacks picked her up and held her in the crook of his left arm, his heart again shifting in his chest as she responded by putting an arm around his neck and holding on tightly. 'You're going to be all right,' he whispered just for her to hear. 'I have a friend called

Jacob and he'll be doing his very best to get you back with your mum.'

'I miss my mummy,' Anna said in a voice so beseeching Jacks almost surrendered to the tears welling up inside him and he did not trust his voice to speak.

A little boy ran ahead and opened the door to the room to which they had been making their way. Then, as Jacks switched on the lights, revealing an array of coffee tables, couches and armchairs, the other boy ran across the room and switched on the gas log fire, which burst impressively into flames.

Jacks gently placed Anna on an armchair that was much too big for her, asked the other children to find a seat by the fire and then told them what was going to happen next. 'In a minute,' he explained, looking from one shiny little face to another, 'I'll phone a friend of mine and very quickly all sorts of nice people will be here to take care of you.'

'Won't you be here?' a little boy asked.

'No,' Jacks replied. 'I have a promise to keep to Jasmin and we have to go.'

'Why?' the other little boy asked.

'I'm a secret agent,' Jacks replied, thinking that the boys would understand. 'And I have to protect my identity.'

In response the boys nodded wisely at each other and Anna asked. 'Mother won't be coming, will she?'

'We don't like mother,' a little boy stated.

'She hurts us and makes us cry,' the other little girl said.

Jacks flinched. 'She won't ever hurt you again,' he promised. Not ever.' Then fighting emotions he'd never known he possessed, he put Jasmin in charge and left the room ostensibly to make a phone-call.

When Jacks was out of the room, the door closed behind him, he stood for a moment, struggling to gather his scattered emotions, then he rang Jacob. As he did so, he noticed an unfamiliar tremor in his hand; he feared that his normally taut self-control was falling apart.

Jacob answered on the second ring. 'Billy,' he exclaimed with evident concern. 'It's gone five o'clock, I was growing worried.'

'I've had things to do,' Jacks came back, noticing that the tremor had reached his voice. 'Take down this address,' he instructed, and went on to give the location of the house in Wimbledon. 'Tell your people that there are children there and tell them to go in with big guns, the people I met here were carrying Stechkins. When your people get here, to this house, they'll find three bodies scattered about the place and four children in a downstairs room. Make sure you send some care along with the guns, plenty of counsellors and therapists, these kids are going to need lots of help and I'm making you personally responsible for their future well-being. I know you'll be doing your best for all of them but there's a little girl called Anna I want you to *really* try for. She's the one from the video I saw and I've already told her that my friend Jacob will be doing his best to find her mummy.'

'It will be done, Billy,' Jacob assured him. 'I presume you'll be leaving before the police arrive. Shall I see you soon?'

'There's more,' Jacks said as bit by bit he was losing the battle against the emotional demands that were running haywire round his system. 'On the way in I stumbled across a kidnap victim. Her name is Jasmin Sek and I've promised to take her back to her father. Don't mention this one to the police. She's my responsibility.'

'Sek?' Jacob questioned. 'Probably the daughter of Ivan Sek. One of the dissident billionaires. When they left Russia with their fortunes, they left behind fierce, unforgiving enemies.'

'I do that everywhere I go,' Jacks said in a voice that was breaking up. 'How long before the police get here?'

'Twenty, thirty minutes.'

'Right,' Jacks breathed. 'Once I see Jasmin home safe, I'll be in touch, but right now, Jacob, I have to let go of myself, I can't hold on any longer.' He ended the call, rested an arm on the wall, leant his head on the arm and surrendered to the emotions that were tearing him apart.

It had been quite a while since Jacks had cried. Now, as his long-dormant emotions were awakened he shed tears that first celebrated release by leaving one drop at a time and then, as though being pushed by a queue from behind, they left in streams. As the tears flowed unbidden, he still stubbornly tried to control his body but, as the unshed tears of a hundred yesterdays joined the flood, he was overtaken by great, racking sobs, shaking helplessly as he drowned in a well of sorrow.

'Are you OK?' a small voice asked and Jacks looked down through a liquid veil to see Jasmin standing there looking very concerned. When she took his right hand, squeezed it and said, 'It's all right, I cry sometimes,' he was moved again to tears.

'You can use this if you like,' Jasmin said, taking a flower-patterned handkerchief from a coat pocket and offering it to him. 'It's all right to use it, I haven't blown my nose or anything.'

How churlish it would have been of Jacks to decline Jasmin's so thoughtful offer. He graciously accepted the handkerchief and then, all the time being watched closely by a big pair of brown eyes, he used it for the purpose intended. As Jacks dried his eyes, he was aware that he was living out the most wonderful reversal of roles. He would remember tonight for a multitude of reasons but he would first remember it as the night a little girl called Jasmin lent him her handkerchief with which to dry his tears.

There are times when life is truly worth the moment.

When Jacks thought himself sufficiently back under control, with Jasmin still holding his hand, he hunkered down before her and said, 'This is our secret?'

'Of course it is,' Jasmin replied in a tone suggesting she could not imagine it being anything less.

'You're some girl,' Jacks said admiringly as he offered Jasmin back her handkerchief. 'Thanks.'

'You can keep it if you like,' Jasmin offered.

Jacks smiled in the purest of pleasure. 'Thanks again,' he said as he folded the somewhat damp trophy into a pocket. 'Now, we need to get out of here. A quick goodbye to the kids and we're gone.'

Scaredy cat that he was, Jacks would have preferred no goodbyes but he really could not leave without reassuring the children that they would soon be safe for ever. He spoke to them as a group but when he mentioned the fact that his friend Jacob was going to do everything he could do for them, he spoke directly to the little girl called Anna.

The boys understood why Jacks had to leave, the girls were just sad to see him go but all four saw him off with a little wave. 'Bye-bye,' Jasmin said as she waved in turn.

'Bye-bye,' Jacks echoed as he did the same.

*

Hand in hand, Jacks and Jasmin left Rosewood House by a back kitchen door, stepping out into a dawning, dull, grey day. They walked round the house to where Jacks had originally emerged from the trees. The binoculars that he had left behind marked the spot. He picked them up and he and Jasmin made their way into the sparse, leafless wood. The earlier flurry of snow had dried to a thaw, making the ground slippery. When Jasmin slipped for a second time, Jacks gave her the binoculars to hold, picked her up in both arms and carried her the rest of the way.

The Audi sat where he had left it. He was about to put Jasmin safely into the passenger seat when she whispered, 'Look.'

Jacks followed her pointing finger and saw the headlights of a line of vehicles approaching Rosewood House by way of the main gate. Jacks had hated deserting the children and when he distinguished the ambulances, the police cars and sundry other vehicles, he felt the most wonderful sense of relief.

'The children will be rescued now,' he said as he got into the car.

'You rescued them first,' Jasmin reminded him as she fastened her seat belt.

'It's who rescues you last who matters most,' Jacks responded as he switched on the Audi and backed out of the field without switching on any lights. 'They're the ones who do the real rescuing.'

'I don't believe you,' Jasmin said firmly.

'Would I tell you fibs, Jasmin?' he questioned drily. 'The sweetest girl I ever met? Your dad's going to be absolutely delighted to have *you* back home safe. He'll rescue you last and then you'll know what I mean. With me, it's for the moment; your dad will rescue you for life. And if we're to get to him, I need to know where he lives.'

'Hampstead Heath,' Jasmin stated.

'Where else?' Jacks questioned drily, pleased to hear that he was sounding his old self.

All that emotion would tear your heart out.

CHAPTER TWELVE

Hampstead Heath is situated in north London and Jacks decided that the most direct route there was by way of Woodford, then on through Tottenham. A glance at the dash clock told him it was 6.15 a.m., light was invading the land, the world was awakening around him and he smiled to think that he was driving off into a sunrise. It had been a while since he had been up all night.

'What's your name?' Jasmin suddenly questioned.

'My name's Billy Jacks,' Jacks responded. 'Most people call me Mister Jacks but you can call me Billy.'

'Billy,' Jasmin echoed. 'I don't know anyone else with that name.'

'There's not too many of me around,' Jacks came back.

'And are you really a secret agent?' Jasmin asked. 'Like James Bond?'

'Not really,' Jacks answered with a grin. 'He's a much better dresser than I am. I'm just me. I'm secret but I'm my own agent. I help a friend out now and again but I'm not an official agent.'

Jasmin smiled knowingly. 'I understand,' she said. 'But you *really* are a secret agent, aren't you?'

How Jacks smiled. 'OK,' he conceded. 'I'm a secret agent. Who am I to argue with the brave Jasmin?'

Jacks kept the banter going but there was a part of his mind that dwelt on a darker subject. Ever since he had left Rosewood House he had been a man who knew he was driving into a trap; the trap had not been designed to catch him but that was what it was going to do. The Red Mafia had kidnapped Jasmin and they had not done so on sudden impulse. Before the kidnap, there would have been much reconnaissance done, much intelligence gathered. Since the kidnap they would have been watching Jasmin's father to make sure that he did not contact the police. The days of parking across the road and watching with binoculars had long gone. They would be watching now courtesy of the Hampstead house internal security system, which meant they would see him coming the moment he drove in through the front gate.

From there, with the car number as a starting point, they would learn what there was to know about William John Cranston. There was not a lot to learn but it would be more than enough for Rasputin to aim Catharine in the right direction. Rasputin would figure out what had gone on down at Rosewood House and would then send her after him for reasons of his own. In order to test his reasoning, Jacks diverted the conversation with Jasmin and began by being clever. 'I bet you've been on holiday recently,' he suggested.

'How did you know that?' a surprised Jasmin asked.

'A lucky guess.' Jacks sidestepped. 'And who exactly went along?'

'My dad and Elizabeth, my nanny,' Jasmin replied. 'There were two men; Dad's bodyguards, I think, but they didn't come back with us.'

Jacks could imagine why. 'You didn't mention your mother,' Jacks pointed out.

'My mummy died when I was little,' Jasmin explained matter of factly. 'She fell off her horse.'

'I'm sorry to hear that,' Jacks responded.

'She was never there very much,' Jasmin said sadly. 'She was always away riding horses somewhere. But I still miss her sometimes. It isn't fair.'

'You're not the first to make such an observation on life,'

Jacks responded. 'But according to a poet friend of mine, life is fair in its own way.'

Jasmin pulled a face. 'What do you mean?'

'I'll tell you,' Jacks answered. 'I won't bore you with the whole poem. It's the last verse that concerns us. You listening?'

'Of course I am, Billy.'

'After much discussion on life,' Jacks began, 'My friend closed the poem with this verse:

> *Life is unfair, and that's a fact.*
> *We have all had our backs to the wall.*
> *But, in being unfair,*
> *Life favours none,*
> *And is fairly unfair to us all.'*

'How can you be fairly unfair?' Jasmin wanted to know.

Jacks smiled all over his face. 'I think it's what they call an oxymoron, but please don't ask me why they call it that. I think being fairly unfair means that we all get our fair share of bad news, but it also means that we get our fair share of good news. The bad news was that you were kidnapped, the good news is that you'll soon be back with your dad.'

'I can't wait to see him,' Jasmin declared.

'He's going to be delighted to see you,' Jacks predicted. 'Now, tell me about your house,' he invited. 'Is it a big house?'

'It's massive,' Jasmin answered emphatically. 'A lot of the rooms are empty but it's great for playing hide and seek. My friends and I have lots of fun when they visit.'

'I like hide and seek, it's my favourite game,' Jacks confessed. 'I've been playing it all my life ... and your big house, does it have a wall round it with an electronic gate?'

'Yes,' Jasmin replied. 'But it's all right, Billy. I know the code, I'll let us in when we get there.'

'That's good to know,' Jacks said with a smile for fate. 'And when we get in, are there lots of security cameras?'

'Trillions,' Jasmin answered. 'My dad likes to keep an eye on me when I'm playing in the gardens.'

'And inside the house?' Jacks asked.

'I know there's one on the big landing,' Jasmin said. 'I practise my dancing in front of it, then afterwards my dad gives me a copy of the film so as I can watch myself and see my mistakes.'

There was no doubt about it, Jacks thought as he negotiated some heavy traffic on Tottenham High Street, no doubt whatsoever, he was driving into a trap.

What to do about it? That was the question.

He could duck, he could sidestep. All he had to do was break a promise to the little girl sitting so trustingly beside him. He could drop Jasmin off close to home and let her walk the rest of the way. There were a hundred ways to duck this one but Jacks could not imagine himself so cowardly that he would betray a cross-your-heart promise to the little girl with the big brown eyes just so that he could go into hiding. He had given her his promise that he would see her safely back to her father and in promising so, how could he now do less?

That was the romantic reason for Jacks's driving into the trap, the deeper reason was much darker.

For a long time now Jacks had walked hand in hand with Lady Death, challenging her to protect him or to take him. It was inevitable that she would take him one of these times and if today was the time, so be it. It was a bit late in the game now for him to knowingly evade his enemies. He had not lied to Jasmin when he said he had been playing hide and seek all his life; what he had not told her was that he did not like the hiding but that he really enjoyed the seeking. This was a Red Mafia operation. Once he was identified by those watching the Hampstead house, they would pass on his identity and whereabouts to Rasputin, who would pass it on to Catharine. Catharine would then set out to hunt him down not knowing that it was in fact *he* who was hunting her down. The poor woman didn't stand a chance.

Jacks was confident; first, because he believed in his own capacity; second, he was confident because he believed he had the edge. Rasputin would learn enough to send Catharine out after him but Rasputin did not know that Catharine was already expected to turn up at any given moment or that, right now, Jacob was trying to find her and, with any luck, had found her by now.

Jacks was expecting Catharine to be waiting somewhere for him when he eventually returned to the Lewisham flat and, in expecting her, he believed he could outthink her all the way.

He did not care how good Catharine's reputation said she was, she was not in his class. Catharine was a mere assassin, he was a natural born survivor.

Surviving was what he did best.

After a bit of a hold-up in Hornsey, Jacks reached Hampstead Heath and then followed Jasmin's directions until he found himself outside the Hampstead house. Jasmin leaned out of her window, spoke a code into an electronic receiver and, like magic, the huge steel gate before them slowly opened wide.

'Open, Sesame,' Jacks said, smiling to himself as he passed through the gate. As he made his way up the drive, he was thinking on how best to play things. The game was to act as though he was quite unaware of being observed and always to speak bearing anyone who might be listening in mind. By the time he pulled up outside the front entrance he had a pretty good idea of what to do next.

'I'm so excited,' Jasmin said as Jacks put on the hand-brake. 'I knew you would keep your promise.'

'You did?' Jacks gave a small smile.

'Of course I did,' Jasmin said before she was diverted by the front door of the house being opened. As a man in a dressing-gown, in the company of a dark-haired woman dressed for the day, emerged; she threw open the car door and ran to greet them. Jacks stayed where he was and watched the wonderful reunion as, with the woman looking on, the man swept Jasmin up into his arms and she held on to him as though he was a lifebelt. The woman kissed Jasmin on a cheek and ruffled her hair and when at last all eyes turned to him he got out off the car and approached the trio of expectant faces.

Holding Jasmin in the crook of his left arm the man, with tears in his eyes, held out his right hand. As Jacks accepted it and his hand was firmly shaken, the man said, 'I'm over-whelmed, sir. I'm overwhelmed.'

'My good deed of the day,' Jacks responded lightly. He broke the handshake and gently chivvied everyone into the house. 'No questions,' he continued as they entered a huge living room. 'Jasmin will tell you all about it later. For now, I want you to listen to me. Then, when you've listened, I want you to do exactly what I tell you to do. Your daughter is home safe but you are all in great danger. I don't know whether Jasmin has been missed yet, but when she is her kidnappers are going to be unhappy people. They'll be honour-bound to come after you and next time they won't settle for just kidnapping your daughter.'

'They'll kill me,' Ivan Sek said as he passed Jasmin on to the dark-haired woman, who led her off somewhere. 'Once they had got their money they would have done that anyway.'

'Good,' Jacks responded. 'I'm glad to hear that you're wise to your situation. They'll hunt you down then kill you. So here's what you do. You pack the family jewels, then the three of you get in one of the big cars outside and get out of here. Next thing you do is lay your hands on some cash and throw away your credit cards. Get rid of the car, buy something less ostentatious for cash from a second-hand car dealer and then get lost in some hotel in the wilderness until you sort things out. Never come back to this house and, next time around, forget that you're a billionaire. Aim middle-market, change your name and send Jasmin to a school where she's not known as the daughter of Ivan Sek. If you want to survive, practise anonymity, being anonymous is the best disguise ...'

As the woman and Jasmin came back into the room carrying a tray of cups and coffee, Jacks tailed off, smiled to see Jasmin drinking orange juice through a straw. He smiled again when the woman offered him a coffee.

'This is Elizabeth,' Sek said.

'The nanny?' Jacks questioned, although he had already figured that the attractive, dark-haired woman was more than that to Jasmin's father and that he was more to her than a mere employer. 'Then take good care of Jasmin,' he advised. 'And you can begin by packing a bag for her and yourself. You're getting out of here.'

In response, Elizabeth looked at Sek. 'Bring the minimum,' he instructed before turning back to Jacks and saying, 'I know you said no questions, but I would dearly love to know the name of the man who returned to me my precious Jasmin.'

Jacks was about to betray his identity to anyone listening in but Jasmin beat him to it. 'This is Mister Jacks, Dad,' she announced with evident pride. 'But I can call him Billy.'

The wonderful irony sliced through Jacks like a silken scythe and he smiled as he looked at Sek and confirmed Jasmin's declaration by saying, 'That's me, Billy Jacks. Now I really do suggest you get out of here. I'll watch your backs until then.'

'Thank you,' Sek said from the bottom of his heart. 'I

would not insult you by offering a reward but I will say that I owe you more than my life and if I can ever be of assistance, I am yours to call upon.'

'You see your daughter,' Jacks asked, pointing at the smiling Jasmin. 'You see that smile? That's reward enough for me. Take care of her.'

'I shall do so every day of my life,' Sek swore.

'A girl as brave and charming as Jasmin deserves no less,' Jacks asserted, touched to the heart as Jasmin blessed him with a smile that shone just for him.

And how he smiled in return.

CHAPTER THIRTEEN

In the basement of the mafia safe house in Golders Green, north London, the two mafiosi observing the Hampstead house watched wonderingly as a screen before them displayed a black Audi pulling up at the front gate. When they saw Jasmin Sek, their kidnap victim, lean out of the passenger door window to press the gate security code their wonder evolved into astonishment. They did not get a good look at the man who was driving but, as they followed the car up the driveway on another screen, they noted the registration number and passed it on to the security section on the first floor with instructions to check it out quickly.

As they watched the family reunion on the doorstep of the house the watchers tried to figure out how such an event had come to pass. They had been watching the house since before the actual kidnap and they were one hundred per cent certain that Ivan Sek had contacted no one on the outside. And even if he had mastered ESP and reached help by way of the spirit world there was not a chance that he knew where his daughter was being held.

By the time the reunited family moved into the house, the security section had passed on the information gathered from the Audi number plate. When the watchers got their first good look at the man who had delivered the girl, they knew they were looking at a man called William John Cranston who lived in Lewisham, south London. The name meant nothing to them but when, a few minutes later, they heard Jasmin Sek introduce the man as Mister Jacks, they heard a name that set their hearts beating faster. There was not a man in the entire organization who did not know the name Mister Jacks.

The Chief had put the word out on Jacks and a big reward awaited the man or men who located him. With such an incentive, the watchers did not hesitate in passing the information on to Amsterdam.

They first contacted Rasputin via satellite phone and then by way of computer, transmitting the images they were receiving from inside the Hampstead house.

The watchers had no idea as to how Mister Jacks had located and then rescued Jasmin Sek but it did not take

Rasputin long to figure out how it had happened. The way he interpreted events, Jacks did not go to Rosewood House to rescue Jasmin Sek, he went there to investigate a honey trap and had come across her by chance. It did not really matter how Jacks had found his way to Rosewood House but since he had, he had undoubtedly brought it tumbling down. The fact that he was still alive meant that he had killed whoever was there.

Rosewood House would undoubtedly lead to the house in Wimbledon and Rasputin suspected that right now his carefully constructed spy ring was being taken apart by a man called Jacob. Jacks was almost certainly doing a job for Jacob and it now appeared that not only was he, Rasputin, going after Mister Jacks, Mister Jacks was already coming at him. Not only had Jacks brought down a British spy network that had taken years to build, in rescuing Jasmin Sek he had cost the organization a hundred million dollars.

Watching Jacks on the computer console, sitting there on a couch in the Hampstead house casually drinking coffee, Rasputin was not fooled for a moment. There was not a chance that Jacks did not know he was under observation. Jacks was a pro, he would have known before arriving at the house that the place would be under surveillance and though it might have appeared that Jasmin Sek had betrayed his name in all innocence, in fact she had done so with his foreknowledge and probably at his request.

Watching Jacks sit there, giving Ivan Sek advice on anonymity, Rasputin thought that Jacks was taunting him. Even in the business, Jacks was an unusual character and Rasputin was quickly coming to understand al-Qaeda's desire to see him dead; it was not so much what Jacks did personally, it was the havoc he left in his wake.

Rasputin did not believe that Jacks would betray his position only to choose then to run away from it. In pursuit of his well-documented death wish, Jacks had thrown down a 'come and get me' challenge and Rasputin figured that Jacks would go on to the Lewisham location, where he would prepare for the arrival of the assassin or assassins sent to kill him.

Jacks was a first-class player, but this time round he was playing one step behind the game. What Jacks did not know was that when he got back to Lewisham he would find an assassin already awaiting his arrival. With this in mind Rasputin rang Catharine in London on her secure landline.

'The target has been located,' he said when Catharine answered.

'Where?' Catharine wanted to know.

'Right now he's in a house on Hampstead Heath but he can be found soon in Lewisham,' Rasputin replied, going on to give Catharine all the information on Jacks that had been gathered.

'Lewisham is just around the corner,' Catharine said.

'Are you prepared?' Rasputin asked.

'Totally,' Catharine responded.

'Then go and kill him,' Rasputin instructed. 'This has become personal. Overnight, Mister Jacks has cost us dearly. When you do kill him, kill him twice, once in your name and once in mine.'

'It will be my pleasure,' Catharine declared.

In the al-Qaeda safe house in Muswell Hill, north London, the agent listening to the goings-on inside Catharine's flat in the Elephant and Castle first recorded her conversation with Rasputin and then transcribed all the relevant information on to paper. When he had done so, he located the Lewisham address on a computer map of London and printed out the most direct route there.

His task completed, the agent gathered together the information he had acquired and took it upstairs to the killer waiting in the attic. The agent worked for al-Qaeda intelligence and spent most of his life sitting before a computer screen. He had never even heard a shot fired in anger, much less fired one, and the assassin codenamed Mithka aroused in him as much curiosity as revulsion. The most interesting thing about Mithka the killer was that he looked just like any ordinary male Caucasian. There was no blood to be seen on his hands, no brand on his forehead to mark him as a killer but this was a man who had killed fighting side by side with the Taliban in Afghanistan, this was the man destined to kill the infamous Mister Jacks. This was a man who commanded respect.

Mithka accepted the information with the relief of a man at long last greeting the arrival of Godot. His evident pleasure at being given the location of the man he was waiting to kill disturbed the agent and he watched in strange fascination as the ever silent Mithka read the details, glanced briefly at the route print-out, got off the bed, slipped on a coat and then made a rather large, nickel-plated automatic fitted with a sound suppressor disappear within its folds.

From the attic the agent led Mithka downstairs. As he gave him the keys to a BMW parked in the backyard he made the mistake of wishing him good luck.

'Luck?' Mithka questioned, giving the agent a chilling look. 'Allah will guide me.'

When Mithka had gone the agent returned to his ground-floor office and contacted Siff in Amsterdam, letting him know that the target had been located and that Operation Mithka was up and running.

Siff was delighted to hear the news. After ordering the agent to close down his side of the operation he terminated the call as a man feeling very pleased with the way his plan was progressing.

At this very minute two highly trained professional assassins were on their way to kill Mister Jacks. It would look better if Jacks were killed by Mithka rather than by Catharine, but it did not really matter who killed the hated enemy. What mattered was that Mister Jacks ended the day by being dead.

Jacks was a man whose death was long overdue.

The man everyone seemed intent on killing was halfway through his second cup of black coffee when Ivan Sek, Elizabeth and Jasmin, carrying holdalls and a suitcase, returned to the living room.

'All set?' Jacks asked, abandoning his coffee and getting swiftly to his feet. 'Then let's go.' He led the way to the front door and then out into a dull, dank morning.

Jacks hated goodbyes and he was not at all looking forward to parting from Jasmin, the little girl whose handkerchief he carried in a pocket. There was a certain sadness about him as he hunkered down before her and said, 'It's been great to meet you. You're a girl I'll never forget.'

'Won't I see you ever again?' Jasmin asked in a plaintive little voice.

'You never know,' Jacks said with a smile. 'We might just bump into each other. But, for now, we both need to disappear for a while. Your dad'll take care of you, and you take care of your dad.'

Jasmin nodded and then took Jacks by surprise as she threw her arms around him, holding on really tight as she said that she would miss him lots and lots.

Rather awkwardly, discomfited by the fact that Jasmin's father and Elizabeth were looking on, Jacks returned the hug and assured her that *he* would miss her.

When Jacks broke the hug, he was surprised yet again when Elizabeth grasped his upper arm, kissed him on a cheek and said, 'God bless you. You're a good man.'

'I know people who would give you an argument there,' Jacks responded with a grin. 'But I appreciate the thought.' He gave Elizabeth's upper arm a squeeze in return. 'You and Jasmin take care of each other.'

As Elizabeth and Jasmin walked hand in hand to the Mercedes, Jacks turned to Ivan Sek and said, 'Some advice I couldn't give you inside the house. Throw away all your mobile phones. Never sign a contract, buy the pay-as-you-go variety, they're as safe as you can get.'

Sek said that he would.

'And at the next place you get,' Jacks continued, 'don't install a high tech security system. The cameras you think are protecting you can be turned against you. That's how the mafia has been watching you. Don't look, because they're watching us right now but they can't hear what we are saying.'

Sek did not look but his eyebrows rose. 'They could hear us inside the house?' he asked in alarm.

'Almost certainly,' Jacks advised. 'They probably bugged the place when you were on holiday.'

'But that means they know who you are,' Sek said.

'They have always known who I am,' Jacks told him. 'What it means is that they now know where to find me. But don't concern yourself, I knew long before I got here that they would learn as much.'

'Then why did you come?' asked a surprised Sek.

'Perhaps because of a promise I made your little girl,' Jacks answered. 'Or perhaps because I didn't really care. The mafia and I are already at war and the only way I can get to them is to let them come after me. Don't spare it a thought; they don't know it, but they're walking into a trap. Now get out of here. You'll need to lead the way, I don't have a key for the front gate.'

Sek looked at Jacks for a long moment. When he had read whatever it was he saw in Jacks's eyes, he again offered him his right hand. As Jacks accepted it and they firmly shook hands, he said. 'It would need to be said, sir. You're a remarkable man.'

'In relation to whom?' Jacks asked with a small smile. Then he broke the handshake, turned abruptly away and made for his Audi.

When the Mercedes pulled out Jacks pulled out behind it. All the way down the drive he was treated to the sight of Jasmm's little face smiling at him out of the back window. When they passed through the gate and the Mercedes turned left as he turned right, she gave him a parting wave that he returned all the way from his heart.

In his day Jacks had parted from more than one female but this time round, he could not do so with an indifferent shrug and a smile for fate; this time round the object of his affection was taking a bit of his heart with her.

The sad thoughts came and went but, very quickly, Jacks turned his mind to what lay ahead. He had a choice of routes that would take him back to Lewisham and he decided to go by way of Finsbury and then on to the Rotherhithe tunnel. This was the quickest, most direct route and not only was he a man anxious to learn his fate; Lady Death was waiting in Lewisham and he was not a man to intentionally keep a lady waiting. Certainly not one he held in such high esteem.

Lady Death is the ineluctable assassin; come the end, she kills us all.

No exceptions.

CHAPTER FOURTEEN

As Leanna drove, Catharine used the London A-Z that came with the rented Mercedes and found the way to the Lewisham location, which turned out to be a three-storey block of private flats.

Catharine told Leanna where to park, got out of the car and walked round the flats checking them as she went. The front entrance displayed the street number she had been given but there was no indication of different flat numbers, name tags or individual doorbells The downstairs flat had that unlived-in look about the windows, with the closed curtains, and when she checked through a gap she saw a bare floor with a couple of boxes stacked by a wall. The middle-floor flat had similarly closed curtains but the top-floor flat had open curtains and a couple of windows were slightly ajar. She figured that this was one of Jacob's safe houses that he used to store whatever need storing while the top floor housed his pet killer, Mister Jacks.

As Catharine walked round the back of the flats, she smiled to see the tower blocks with their boarded-up windows looming before her. As she moved on, she had already worked out roughly where to position herself for the kill.

Catharine figured that time was on her side, it was quite a way to Hampstead Heath. Mister Jacks must be running at least forty-five minutes behind. In Prague she had once set up a hit in eleven minutes. Admittedly she had needed to kill the young couple who were occupying the flat from where she took her shot, but when the target's taxi from the airport pulled up outside the hotel she was waiting to greet him with a head shot. Three quarters of an hour was more than enough time to prepare for a hit.

In Catharine's mind, Jacks was already a dead man.

On returning to the Mercedes, Catharine had Leanna drive round to the condemned tower blocks, selected the one she wanted and then again told her where to park.

'I could be an hour or more,' Catharine said as she collected a metal briefcase from the back seat. 'So don't be getting up to any mischief when I'm gone. If anything happens that you think I should know about, you know the signal.'

'Three loud blasts on the horn,' Leanna responded. 'I'll watch your back like you've trained me to do and I'll be here when you return. Is this really the last time?'

'Sadly, yes,' Catharine replied. 'But I shall go out on a high note. Half the world wants Mister Jacks dead but it is I who is going to kill him.' As she got out of the car she was a woman resolute in her intent.

As Leanna watched Catharine disappear into a tower block her concern grew. If Catharine was retiring did that mean the end of their relationship? Catharine had not been the same since her return from Amsterdam, not so caring, not so attentive and certainly not as loving.

As Leanna wondered how she would survive without Catharine being there to take care of her, and seeking assurance that someone, somewhere, loved her, she retrieved her mobile phone from where it was hidden in her handbag, switched it on and then rang her big sister in Prague.

Catharine had said an hour at least and Leanna reasoned that she had plenty of time.

As Catharine climbed the cold, stone steps to the fourth floor of the damp, decaying tower block, an old excitement was reborn within her. After all the boring, harmless targets she had brought down on instruction, she was going to end her career by bringing down the man recognized to be the most ruthless in the business. Catharine knew that she herself was a hitter of repute. She believed that she had always been better than Mister Jacks, but she was working in a male-dominated business and the kudos always went to the man. Let it be seen how it went down when word spreads that Mister Jacks had been taken down by a woman. It was well known that the female was the deadlier of the species and she would be the living proof.

In bringing down Mister Jacks, the name Catharine would enter the annals of folklore.

The fourth floor proved to be the perfect choice. As Catharine walked along the walled landing, the target block of flats came into view and she kept walking until she stood looking directly down on it, taking in the large window with its partly open side windows and its wide-open curtains.

A door behind Catharine, though secured by a Yale lock, was hanging off its hinges. She gave it a hard push, then closing the door behind her, wedging it tight, she stepped into a smelly, rotting world of damp cardboard boxes, last year's newspapers, discarded syringes and a mouldy mattress that had long since lost any comfort it had ever had to offer.

Treading carefully, Catharine went into the kitchen and found the window she had identified from the outside.

Someone had already smashed out the panes of glass and the originally secure outside boarding had been reduced to one slat and a central bar that left her with an uninterrupted view of the target flat below.

Feeling so utterly alive, Catharine laid her metal briefcase on the rusty draining board, clicked it open, slowly raised the lid and then performed a ceremony she had performed many times before. As the surgeon has his instruments of life, she had her instrument of death, its pieces all neatly laid out, each in its own compartment inside the case. As she set about putting them together the sensations were so pleasurable they were almost erotic.

The case contained a specially modified, segmented Dragunov sniper rifle and Catharine began by attaching the stock to the barrel; the satisfying loud click as the two joined perfectly sent a shiver up her back.

The Dragunov came with a PSO-1, 4 x 24 scope and a PSO-1 silencer. When Catharine had fitted them into place she raised the rifle, fitted the butt with its cheek pad into her right shoulder and focused on the target flat's window and beyond it into a room, where the end of what she thought was a futon bed was revealed. Beyond was an open central door that opened on to a corridor which, no doubt, led to the way in.

Catharine reckoned it was a 400-metre shot, adjusted the

THE HUNT FOR MR JACKS

scope to allow for a two-minute arc, then concluded the ceremony by turning the harmless wood and metal in her hand into an instrument of death.

The modified Dragunov came with only two bullets; the first, Catharine put down the barrel. The second bullet came in a specially designed clip and as she clicked it into place the resulting sound spoke to her of finality. It was a very contented woman who eventually raised the armed Dragunov to her shoulder. Then, standing back from the kitchen window in order to get the required angle, she sighted on the window below.

The ceremony over, all Catharine had to do now was wait and she was an expert at waiting. She had once lain for five hours on a snow-covered Moscow rooftop waiting for a target to show herself. Besides, she was Russian and it was a well-known fact that only the Russians have the patience it takes to be a great sniper, a fact proven by the way Mossad had lured so many ex-Russian military snipers into their ranks.

Standing there in that dank, smelly kitchen, Catharine was not at all concerned about the waiting. What was another half-hour or so when she felt as though she had been waiting for this one all her life?

After this one, she could retire in grace and glory.

*

After three years of fighting in Helmand with the Taliban, Mithka found it strange to again be behind the wheel of a car but his past experience coupled with his immaculate reflexes saw him through and, very quickly, he was dealing with the London traffic as though he had been doing so every day of his life.

Mithka was feeling good. The wait in the safe house had been the hard part; from here until the end it was looking like an easy ride. With Mister Jacks having to come from Hampstead, barring accidents, Mithka was pretty certain that he would be first to reach the Lewisham location. Once he did, it would not take five minutes to set up the kill.

Mithka had decided to kill Mister Jacks the way Mister Jacks liked to kill them, up close and by putting a bullet in their heads. It was a matter of record that although Jacks had killed many in the field no one was known to have got even one shot off at him. Jacks had beaten them all to the draw or ambushed them at the pass, but this time round it was he who was walking into the ambush and no one on earth is faster than a 9 mm bullet fired from a Heckler & Koch USB9.

Mithka's route took him over Southwark Bridge, and on to a route for the Old Kent Road, once there, it was a straight run into Lewisham High Street.

On reaching there, Mithka located the target address. No black Audi was parked anywhere round the block of flats and he read this to mean that Mister Jacks had yet to arrive. In this belief he took the first right turn and eventually ended up parking in a space at the end of a double row of lock-up garages that ran adjacent to the flats.

Mithka parked, then got out of the BMW a man with a mission to fulfil.

Out of the corner of an eye, Catharine saw the roof of a black car that was pulling into the lock-up garages. She thought it could be an Audi, so she brought the Dragunov round and sighted on the car and on the man getting out of the driver's door. She could only see him from the chest up but the clean-shaven man with the brown eyes and brown hair wearing a dark coat fitted the description given by Rasputin and Catharine thought it could be Mister Jacks. At one point she had a clear shot at the back of the man's head but she did not want to kill the target until she was certain that she was killing the right man.

When the man disappeared from view Catharine turned the Dragunov back on the target window, sighting on the central open door that led out to the entrance. She stood as though carved in stone as she anticipated making the finest kill she ever had made or would ever make again.

A pair of black-leather-shod feet came into view first, dark trousers and a pair of knees were followed by the bottom of a coat. When Catharine saw that the man's right hand was holding a silenced gun all concern about killing the wrong man fled as she sighted her weapon briefly on his face, then pulled the trigger twice in rapid succession.

The first bullet to leave the Dragunov was a 7N14, a 151-grain projectile with a lead core that spun through the air at a speed of 2,723 feet per second. When it hit the double-glazed window, it smashed a hole in each pane before being deflected and going on to hit the target just below his left collar bone.

The second bullet to leave the Dragunov was a 7N1, a steel-jacketed projectile with an air pocket, steel core and a lead knocker in the base designed for MTE, maximum termination effect. Following the same trajectory as bullet number one, travelling straight at the same 2,723 feet per second, unhindered by glass, it hit the target between the eyes, the force sending him hurtling backwards as it punched a hole in his skull, tore away the back of his head and sprayed the walls with his flesh and blood.

The double-shot kill took no longer than a split second but it qualified as the most exciting moment of Catharine's life. Shivers were running up her back and she felt a certain ache down there as she dismantled the Dragunov and put it back in the case, securing the locks with a great sense of completion.

She had just killed Mister Jacks. In believing so, pride was almost bursting out of Catharine. She left the smelly flat a woman as content with life as she ever had been.

Yet again, she had done what so many men had failed to do.

As soon as she saw Catharine approach, Leanna started the Mercedes. Then, when Catharine was safely in the passenger seat, she drove away to Lewisham High Street. As she negotiated the late-morning traffic, she was waiting for Catharine to say something and she was somewhat disconcerted when Catharine chose to speak not to her, but into her secure mobile phone.

Flushed with excitement, Catharine wanted the world to know of her great accomplishment. She began spreading the news by phoning Rasputin in Amsterdam.

'The target is down,' she stated proudly.

'Excellent,' Rasputin responded sincerely. 'Did he die well?'

'Like a warrior,' Catharine replied. 'He went down with a gun in his hand.'

'Good,' Rasputin judged. 'As he was, he deserved no less. Where are you going now?'

'Back to the flat, then on to Paris,' Catharine answered. 'I'll drop the Hertz car off at Heathrow and then catch an afternoon flight. I'll call you when I get there. If you still think I should retire, it's time I started thinking about what to do with the rest of my life.'

Rasputin smiled down the phone. 'I'm sure I could find something for you to do,' he said encouragingly. 'I know I have never treated you with the respect you deserved. After today, this has changed. Did you know that Mister Jacks is your forty-seventh successful mission? Forty-seven, and you never once missed. My respect for you is long overdue.'

Already flushed with success, Catharine glowed with a different pride. She had been seeking Rasputin's respect since day one; the pleasure she felt to have at last won that respect almost outshone the pleasure she had felt at the kill.

Almost, but not quite.

CHAPTER FIFTEEN

As Catharine and Leanna left Lewisham by way of the High Street, Jacks entered by way of the back streets and made for the condemned tower blocks that stood at the rear of his flat. If Catharine was awaiting his return, then it was pretty certain that she would be waiting there. Over the years he had watched the deterioration of the tower blocks and he had known for a long time now that they posed a threat. How often had he encouraged his death wish by standing at the back window, drinking coffee while daring someone to take him down. He not only knew what particular tower block Catharine would choose, he had a pretty good idea of from which broken window she would shoot.

Catharine would not know that Jacks was expecting her to be waiting for him. If she did she would be using a different tactic but, as things stood, she would use her favoured long gun and, being the prime target he was, she would want to bring him down with her famous double-shot. Reputations are dangerous in that they can work against you as much as for you and in knowing Catharine's so well, he knew enough to outthink her all the way.

When Jacks reached the tower blocks, he parked well away from the one he wanted, checked his Ivor Johnson and then went to hunt down and kill the woman who was intent on doing as much to him.

The first thing Jacks looked for was the out-of-place parked car. When he did not spot one he began to wonder whether he was perhaps reading things wrongly. He often cut through the area when walking to the paper shop and from what he saw nothing was out of place; the only car on view was the burnt-out shell of a Rover that had been falling apart for a good month.

When Jacks reached the block he wanted, he climbed to the fourth floor and, Ivor Johnson at the ready, walked along the landing. When his flat came into view on his right, he slowed his pace, carefully checking each door and broken window as he went. When he reached the window from which the cleanest shot could be made, he was disappointed to find no one waiting with a long gun.

Jacks checked a couple more of broken windows, but by

then he was really starting to believe he had got it all wrong. Perhaps Catharine did know she was expected and had chosen not to make the predictable move. Perhaps she was right now waiting in his flat, ready to kill him with a handgun.

With such thoughts Jacks stood back from the landing wall and looked down at the window of his flat, but the distance and the pale sunlight being reflected back from the glass prevented him from discerning anything.

It was looking as though Catharine's reputation did not say all there was to say about her and Jacks was a very thoughtful man as he walked back along the landing.

As he made his way down the concrete stairs, putting the Ivor Johnson back inside his coat, he was wondering what he would do if he did not find Catharine waiting for him indoors. If she was not there it would be a case of anywhere, any time and it would be back to his being the hunted one.

On returning to the Audi Jacks found it surrounded by a local gang of kids he had often seen on his travels. He smiled when the leader, a boy wearing a black hoody, demanded a tenner in payment for them taking care of his car.

'A tenner?' Jacks questioned with exaggerated disbelief. 'This is a top of the range Audi, don't be so cheap. I reckon thirty quid, that'll give you a fiver apiece.' He handed the notes over to the leader, whose utter surprise spread all over his face. 'I appreciate you taking care of my car.'

'Thanks, mister,' a couple of the kids said as they all gathered round their leader, the man with the money.

'We know you,' one of the kids said.

'You live in the private flats,' a girl said.

How Jacks smiled, and here he had been thinking he was such a big secret. 'Very observant,' he said. 'So tell me, you seen any other strange cars around this morning?'

'The Merc,' one of the boys said.

'A grey Mercedes 220 SL,' another boy qualified. 'Rented. There was a Hertz sticker in the back window.'

'It had blacked-out windows,' a girl added.

'Anyone in it?' Jacks asked.

One of the boys laughed and said, 'A skinny bird with blond hair and a funny accent.'

'We were winding her up and she gave us a tenner to go away,' a girl offered.

I bet she did, Jacks thought as he opened the Audi door. 'How long ago?' he asked.

'Twenty minutes,' the leader answered.

'Thanks, kids,' Jacks said. 'You've done me a right favour here.'

'Are you a villain?' the smallest of the group wanted to know.

'That would depend on who was telling the story,' Jacks replied, smiling wide as he got into the car. 'One man's villain is another woman's hero. Take care, kids. And don't be hustling the blind, you've got to draw your line somewhere.'

As Jacks pulled away, the kids standing respectfully aside, he was trying to figure out what was going on. The skinny bird with the blond hair and funny accent sounded as though she could be Catharine's girlfriend, the failed ballerina, but if she had driven Catharine to the tower blocks why had Catharine not waited to make the hit? It could not possibly be that her nerve had gone and she had called it off. The only thing that made sense was that for one reason or another Catharine decided to change location. The only other place for an ambush was the flat but even that reasoning did not make complete sense. But that was all he had and it was a very thoughtful, confused Jacks who drove away to Lewisham High Street.

Jacks never parked outside his front door and when he pulled into the lock-up garages, he saw a strange black BMW in his usual parking place. He could not see such a car without being reminded of al-Hashashin and his mind was racing as he parked beside it, got out of the Audi and made for the flat.

The flat was pretty secure but Jacks knew that no locked

door was truly secure. He himself had a device in his pocket that would disengage any electronic lock and he assumed the enemy would have something similar.

When Jacks reached the doorstep of the building he took the Ivor Johnson from inside his coat and held it tightly pressed against his side. When he unlocked the door, pushing it wide open, he was prepared to shoot anyone waiting for him in the carpeted hallway. No one was there, neither was anyone waiting on the stairheads and he made it safely to his front door where he checked under the mat to see if the talcum powder had been disturbed. It had not, which meant that either Catharine had stepped over it or that once again he was reading the play wrongly.

When he had checked under the mat, hunkered down, he raised the letterbox millimetre by millimetre, catching his breath when a bloody head came into view and he saw the body of a dead man lying in the lobby.

Quick as you like, Jacks unlocked the door and stepped into the flat, gun held before him. When he saw the window with a hole in it, the silenced H & K USB9 lying by the dead man who had been double shot, he put the scenario together in an instant.

Jacks's pleasure lay in the fact that he had in fact correctly read Catharine's play, she *had* acted as he predicted she would. Only, come the end, she had killed the wrong man. The BMW parked round the corner, together with the H & K, suggested that the dead man was al-Hashashin and it looked as though two assassins out to kill him had got their wires crossed. The dead man was white, he was about the right height, he was dressed similarly to Jacks. Underneath the blood he had brown hair and his wide-open, staring eyes were brown. The description fitted, the location was right; in addition the fact that he was carrying a gun made it not surprising that Catharine had brought him down in the belief that she was killing Mister Jacks.

What a break.

Jacks was a man ever ready to move on at five minutes' notice but it hardly took him as long to throw what he might need for now into a small holdall before smartly leaving the premises, a man once again the hunter.

All he needed to do now was track down the game.

When Jacks had driven clear of the area, he pulled into the side of a road and retrieved his mobile phone. When he switched it on he saw that he had three unread messages. He rang the only person who could have left them.

'Billy,' Jacob replied with evident relief. 'Where are you?'

'Lewisham,' Jacks replied.

'Thank God you've rung me in time,' Jacob responded.

'Don't go near your flat. There is a very good chance that Catharine is waiting for you.'

'I've already been there,' Jacks replied. 'And so has Catharine. She brought down the wrong man.' He went on to tell Jacob about the dead body he had found there. 'It looks like two guns were out to kill me and they walked into each other.'

'My God,' Jacob breathed. 'It would appear that I did not know *everything* that was going on. Any ideas on the dead man.'

'There's a black BMW parked round the corner,' Jacks answered. 'And he was carrying a silenced H & K—'

'Al-Hashashin,' Jacob declared.

'Looks like it,' Jacks agreed. 'The BMW is their company car and H & K are standard issue. You'll need to send the cleaners into the flat and I'm going to need a new base. But right now I need to know where to find Catharine. I presume you've located her.'

'She was easy to find,' Jacob told him. 'Her girlfriend has been regularly using a contract mobile phone and also using credit cards all over town. When the flat was scanned we found at least half a dozen planted listening devices, which we tuned into. I had wondered who else was listening in and now I know. It looks like al-Hashashin gave the job to Rasputin only so that Catharine would lead them to you.'

'Looks that way,' Jacks said. 'Now tell me where I can find Catharine.'

'Just walk away, Billy,' Jacob advised. 'If Catharine believes she has killed you she will have passed the news on to Rasputin who will pass it on to al-Hashashin who will pass it on to al-Qaeda and pretty soon everyone will believe you are dead. Stay dead, Billy. Come in from the cold and I'll see you safe for the rest of your life.'

'I'm not even tempted. Safe is not on my list of things to be,' Jacks responded. 'I like the idea of being dead but the thought of Catharine living on to boast that she was the one who killed me rubs me up the wrong way. Besides, how many dead men get a chance to even the score by killing the one who killed them? I'll come in when I've finished the job. Just tell me where I can find my killer.'

'There's no talking you out of it?' Jacob asked.

'I've already talked myself into it,' Jacks stated. 'So just point me in the right direction.'

'As you wish,' Jacob said. He gave Jacks all the information he had on Catharine and reminded him that she was not alone.

'I'll handle the failed ballerina,' Jacks stated as he started the Audi and made for the location in the Elephant and Castle. 'And stop listening in. I don't want what happens next being broadcast to the nation.'

'It won't be,' Jacob said reassuringly. 'I would advise you to be careful but you have no need of such advice.'

'I don't need advice, I have all I need in a pocket,' Jacks said pointedly. 'I'm switching off, Jacob. Don't try to contact me again. Next time we talk it'll be over a cup of coffee.'

'I'll be waiting,' Jacob promised.

'And I'll be there.' Jacks terminated the call.

CHAPTER SIXTEEN

On the drive back to the Elephant and Castle, still flushed with success, feeling proud, Catharine found herself in a benevolent, forgiving mood and by the time she reached the flat she was considering giving Leanna another chance.

After all, the dear girl was still so young.

There was, perhaps, a lesson that Leanna needed to learn, but then Leanna was very good at learning her lessons. She had yet to forget a lesson once learned. Besides, what with Christmas in Paris just around the corner, this was no time for heartache and drama. With Mister Jacks successfully disposed of, this was a time for celebration and Catharine did not want anything ruining her wonderful sense of accomplishment. She needed someone with whom to share her triumph.

Considering that Leanna had helped her achieve that triumph then Leanna was the one with whom to share it.

The coming New Year would be the time for change.

When Catharine and Leanna entered the flat they were laughing and teasing each other just as they used to in the early days of their relationship. Leanna began to think that she had been imagining any rift between them.

Sometimes she could be so foolish.

There was an hour or so before they needed to leave for Heathrow and Catharine, already erotically stimulated by the kill, dragged Leanna under a shower where she seduced her quite violently while using her to sate her needs and her longings.

With her relationship with Catharine seemingly re-established, Leanna was the happy girl she liked to be; but happiness is a precarious condition and hers did not last *too* long.

The last time Leanna had used her mobile phone, she had been disturbed by a gang of apparently threatening kids. In her panicked hurry to see them off she had returned the phone to her handbag without turning it off. When, as she was the midst of packing, it suddenly rang, the usual melodic tone from the *Nutcracker Suite* sounded to her more like a death knell. That was exactly what it turned out to be.

The alien, ringing phone at once told Catharine everything. 'You stupid bitch, you stupid, stupid bitch,' she hissed, stepping towards Leanna and then viciously slapping her across the face. 'Do you know what you might have done and probably have?' The tone of her question was venomous as Leanna bounced into a wall. 'You've betrayed me, you've fucking betrayed me.' Her appalled disbelief was evident as she approached the cowering, wet-eyed girl.

Leanna was petrified by Catharine's stony look. She had seen Catharine before and after she had killed someone but she had never before seen the killer in Catharine's face; when she did, when she looked into those empty eyes that were looking through her then far beyond, she would have fainted had not Catharine hit her again.

The first time Catharine hit Leanna it had been with a slap generated by anger, the second and last time she hit her it was with a cold, calculated chop to her neck.

It was a blow designed to kill and that was what it did.

Leanna's neck snapped and she slid down the wall like a discarded rag doll, crumpling to the floor where she lay wide-eyed in death, looking as though she could not believe what had just happened to her.

The *Nutcracker Suite* ringtone was still demanding a response. Catharine found the offending mobile phone and switched it off. She then searched Leanna's handbag and was not at all surprised to find a collection of credit cards, one of which had been issued nine months ago. Catharine paled to think that she had been traceable for all that time, while consoling herself with the thought that if one of her many enemies had been on to her for so long, they would have come after her long before now.

Either way, safe or unsafe, Catharine decided that it was time to get out of here.

Almost packed already, Catharine threw what else she might need into the suitcase and left the flat. She avoided using the lift and waited until she was on a stairhead before using her cloned mobile to contact Rasputin once again in Amsterdam.

'Catharine?' Rasputin questioned in reply. 'So soon?'

'There's been a change of plan, Leanna won't be travelling on with me,' Catharine responded. 'I'll be travelling on alone. I'm leaving the flat in a bit of a mess, perhaps you could arrange for it to be cleaned out.'

'Such a parting is long overdue,' Rasputin opined. 'And don't be concerned, the flat will soon be put back in order.'

'When you send the cleaners into the flat,' Catharine advised, 'Send in someone to give the place a sweep. My companion was using a contract mobile phone and credit cards I knew nothing about. It's not likely that the place is bugged because anyone on to me would have put in an appearance by now, but you'd be wise to check it out.'

Rasputin quickly realized that if anyone had been listening in to Catharine they had also been listening in to anything he had said to her over the supposedly secure landline. 'It would seem you may have been careless,' he said.

'My last crime,' Catharine stated. 'My last anything, Rasputin. I'm not going to Paris, I'll decide where I'm going on my way to Heathrow. My retirement starts now; don't expect to hear from me ever again. I know what your idea of retirement can be.'

So saying, Catharine terminated the call and left the building intending to catch a suitable flight out of Gatwick. She could drop the Hertz off at any airport and she felt safer with Rasputin not knowing her starting point. If listening devices were found at the flat Rasputin would be angry, and he was not known to be a forgiving man.

With such thoughts, anxious to be on the move, Catharine almost ran into the underground garage, using a remote to unlock the Mercedes' doors as she approached. She put her suitcase in the boot and then hurriedly got into the car. She was just about to put the key in the ignition when a cold circle of metal that she instantly recognized was pressed into the flesh below her left ear and a voice said, 'Hello, Catharine. I don't care if it's now or then but if you prefer then, move over into the passenger seat. I want to see you face on, and I want you looking at me.'

Faced with such a choice, and with a bit of a struggle, Catharine climbed over the gear stick and into the passenger seat.

'Put the keys on the driving seat and put on your seat belt,' Jacks instructed. 'And then turn this way.'

Catharine did as instructed and then found herself looking along the barrel of a silenced gun into a pair of dark-brown eyes that spoke to her of death. 'Who are you?' she questioned in a tremulous voice.

'I'm the man you think you just killed,' Jacks replied. 'Surely you recognize what I'm pointing at you. You must have heard of the famous Mister Ivor Johnson.'

Catharine knew all about Ivor Johnson and, in her knowledge, her face paled while her heart beat faster in her chest. 'Mister Jacks,' she exclaimed disbelievingly as her whole being was swamped by a terrible, knowing fear the like of which she had never before experienced.

'That's me,' Jacks confirmed. 'Where's your friend, Leanna Korchov, the failed ballerina?'

'Leanna is staying behind,' Catharine replied in a voice dancing on the edge of terror. 'Is that how you got to me?' she asked as her mind fought to find a way out of her impossible situation. 'Through Leanna?'

'As it happens,' Jacks replied, 'I eventually got to you by way of a very observant gang of south London kids. But I didn't come here for a chat, I came to kill you.'

'You're going to kill me?' Catharine questioned fearfully. 'Just like that?'

'There's another way?' Jacks questioned in turn as he pointed the Ivor Johnson directly at her face. He pulled the trigger, shooting her in the centre of her forehead. The force behind the exploding bullet sent her head spinning round but not before it had blown away the back of her head, spraying the window and upholstery with her blood and brains.

The seat belt held Catharine in place but, as her ruined head lolled lifelessly to one side, her bowels moved and the resulting permeating smell of human faeces mixed with that of cordite had Jacks hurriedly picking up the car keys from the driver's seat, putting his gun away inside his coat and leaving the car in one long-held breath, which he did not release until he had used the remote on the key ring to relock the car doors.

An undignified ending, but the manner of Catharine's death did not matter to Jacks; what mattered to him was that she was dead.

And, thanks to her, so was he.

Jacks left the car park, a man suddenly made weary. His

invading tiredness spoke up for itself with a yawn that he fought to stifle, shaking his head in the face of a cold wind, bringing his will into play as he straightened his body, held his head higher while lengthening his stride.

Sleep would come later but for now Jacks had Jacob to visit and he smiled as he wondered exactly where he would end up sleeping. He would never again return to the Lewisham flat, which meant that right now he was technically homeless.

It was a long time since Jacks had found himself in such a situation but he consoled himself with the knowledge that back then getting a bed for the night had been a game of chance. As his life now stood he had a choice of beds, and by the time he reached the parked Audi, he knew exactly where he would spend the night.

At least, he hoped he did.

CHAPTER SEVENTEEN

On previous visits to the Norwood house, Jacob had stood when Jacks entered his office. On this occasion Jacob was already standing and, though he had always greeted Jacks with a handshake, it seemed to Jacks that this handshake was firmer and warmer and he wondered what the occasion was.

'You look exhausted, Billy,' Jacob said with apparent concern.

'That's probably because I am,' Jacks granted, laying the keys to Catharine's rented Mercedes on the desk. 'A shower'll wake me up. I have a way to go before I can call it a night – or should that be call it a day? In the meantime, send someone to the Elephant and have them get rid of the Merc in the underground garage. Catharine's in the passenger seat. She's very dead and she's smelling ripe so tell whoever you send to hold their breath. It's better for me if the body just disappears.'

Jacob nodded in agreement. 'And her friend, the failed ballerina?'

'Fortunately, I didn't have to deal with her,' Jacks replied. 'I think Catharine killed her. All these bodies lying around. How did I ever get involved with such a world?'

'You volunteered,' Jacob reminded him.

Jacks smiled. 'Of course I did,' he agreed ironically. 'Tell me the rest when I've freshened up.' He turned away and made for the shower room. 'Some coffee would be good and I'd trade my cashmere socks for a bacon sarnie.'

As Jacob watched Jacks disappear through a door he wondered, not for the first time, about the man he knew as Billy Jacks. As ever, he could not truly find the words that would encapsulate him in a sentence, but he was certainly a man who could generate wonder.

Had Freud known the complex Jacks, he'd have given up psychiatry in favour of becoming dustman.

Half an hour or so later a much more alive Jacks was seated in Jacob's office drinking strong, black coffee while doing justice to a couple of rounds of bacon sandwiches. As Jacob watched he thought that Jacks was the only man in the world whom he would allow to eat a sandwich in his office, and a *bacon* sandwich at that. But then, Jacob had changed many a rule for Jacks, including the one about not bringing a gun on to the premises. The first time Jacks had done so every alarm in the place was triggered and Jacob's choice then had been either to ask Jacks to surrender his weapon or to invite him into his office for a cup of coffee. To have done less would have shown a mistrust that would have ruined a relationship that was built on the opposite. Since then, Jacob had always switched off the alarm when he saw Jacks arrive.

Jacks had a gift for being the exception to the rule but Jacob had once or twice wondered how Jacks would have reacted if he *had* been asked to surrender his weapon. From what he had learnt about Jacks since, Jacob thought with an inner smile, he'd probably have been so offended, he would have drawn his gun and shot everyone in sight.

'What are you smiling about?' Jacks questioned as he poured himself a fresh mug of coffee.

'I didn't know my smile had reached my face,' Jacob said, now smiling openly.

'It hadn't,' Jacks confirmed. 'I saw it coming. So, tell me about it, Jacob. Did you plug all your leaks?'

'All eleven of them,' Jacob replied. 'Including one in the French embassy and two in the American. And they were not all being blackmailed for paedophilia. Five of them were involved in heavy BDSM, the homosexual variety. The woman among the envelopes from Stockwell favoured a somewhat bizarre form of lesbian bondage.'

'I think I passed through her playground,' Jacks said. 'And they're all banged up. No deals?'

'Only of a kind,' Jacob said, raising a hand to still any anger Jacks might betray. 'They could all be charged with treason but it would be better if the public at large did not learn about the spy ring. Such news would greatly undermine public morale, not to mention faith in the security services. As it is, all eleven will plead guilty to other charges. The paedophiles will be sentenced to life with a thirty-year minimum. The others will end up with ten to fifteen years in a maximum security prison. Is this justice enough?'

'I'd rather I just shot the paedophiles,' Jacks responded. 'But it sounds fair enough to me ... with one exception.'

Jacob raised a questioning eyebrow.

'The woman into lesbian bondage,' Jacks said, a grin hovering. 'Send her to a maximum security prison and she's going to love every minute of her sentence. All those uniforms, crisp white shirts, the rattle of keys, the bars and all those fellow prisoners just queuing up to cater to her needs. You know what they say, one women's hell is another woman's heaven. Isn't justice wonderful?'

'It is indeed,' Jacob agreed. 'And you have more than played your part in bringing it about.'

Jacks ignored the compliment. 'And the kids?' he asked. 'Little Anna?'

'All the children are now in good hands. I have some of my own people closely involved with the carers,' Jacob replied. 'And it is looking good for your little friend. The Moscow police are right now tracking down her mother. Anna was already listed as a kidnap victim and by coincidence, should there be such a thing, they wanted to talk about it with the man we knew as the Snake.'

'If I needed a better reason for killing him than the one I had,' Jacks commented, 'then you just gave me one. Those kids were quite an experience for me, Jacob. They fair tore my heart out.'

'And you made an impression on them,' Jacob told him. 'The police involved in the dawn raid were curious about the man who had originally rescued them but the children told them no more than that you were a really nice man. And they never mentioned that you left Rosewood House with the Sek girl.'

'Good on them,' Jacks declared. 'I was way out of my depth there, Jacob. All that emotion. I don't know how I'd have done it without Jasmin's support. She's some girl.'

'You must have known that the Hampstead house was

under surveillance,' Jacob commented as he gave Jacks a knowing look. 'So why did you knowingly drive into a trap? It was certainly one you could have avoided.'

'I'm sure you've already figured it out, Jacob,' Jacks stated. 'If I hadn't known that the mafia were already on my case, if I hadn't known that Catharine was already hunting me down, then I might have played it differently. With my knowledge I could do no less than draw her out and, in doing so, bear in mind that she didn't know that I knew she was already tracking me. She became the hunted and I became the hunter. Besides, I made a cross-my-heart promise to Jasmin that I would see her home safe to her dad.'

'Catharine did kill someone at your flat,' Jacob reminded him.

'Had she still been waiting for me,' Jacks asserted, 'She never would have got a shot off. I read her play correctly; all she gained by her mistake was another hour of life. Do we know who the dead man is?'

'American,' Jacob answered. 'His prints are on file with the FBI. Homeland militant affiliations by way of his family. Converted to the Muslim faith, met with a mullah with al-Qaeda connections, flew to Paris and subsequently disappeared. Suspected of being an al-Hashashin agent and of fighting with the Taliban in Afghanistan.'

Jacks put the pieces together. 'Then it looks like al-Qaeda

hired the mafia only so that al-Hashashin could tag along. The two hitters must have been ignorant of each other, which turned out to be very good news for me. Am I still officially dead?'

'By now,' Jacob answered, 'there can't be anyone in the business who has not heard that Catharine has killed Mister Jacks. I am doing my bit by leaking a denial, claiming that it was you who killed *her*. My denial will be expected, perhaps, but my supposed disinformation, put with the fact that there are no bodies on display and no Catharine to talk about her triumph, will keep them wondering. Rasputin will *wonder* what has happened to Catharine but he will believe you are dead. He will have informed al-Qaeda and though they will *wonder* what happened to their man, they will believe Rasputin. That is the wonderful secret of this secret world you and I live in, Billy, it is in fact secret. Unless you know all there is to know then you know only what you have been told and, come the end, somewhat ironically, one agent can only take the word of another. More often than not, no proof is offered and no proof is expected. No one will be looking to read of your death in the papers, or hear of it on the TV news. You're dead because Catharine told Rasputin she had killed you. From then on, it's simply a case of the next man believing what he's told. There no doubt will be the mandatory legend about you that says you are still alive but, the fact is, only myself, you and whoever you choose to tell knows for a fact that you are.'

'Great,' Jacks exclaimed. 'But I'm going to need everything, Jacob, birth certificate, national insurance number, all the way up.'

'Of course,' Jacob agreed. 'And you need a new location. Anywhere in mind?'

'Something detached but not too big. Maybe a bungalow.' Jacks replied. 'Out of London, around Brighton possibly. I can always stay at Harry's if I come up to town. I'll need to get the Audi doctored so I'll need to borrow a car for now.'

Jacob opened a drawer, retrieved a set of keys and slid them across the desk. 'I'll have someone from the garage pick up the Audi,' he said. 'There's an Escort parked round the side, use that for now. And then there's your new identity. Any particular name in mind?'

Jacks grinned. 'I'm not vain enough to name myself, Jacob. William John Cranston was christened by a priest in a church, Billy Jacks was christened by a bank-robber at a card-table, it would be nice to get my new name from a spymaster sitting in his den. Keep the William, I've grown used to being Billy. After that, call me what you will, Jacob. By any name I'll still be me.'

'And therein lies your problem,' Jacob said, giving Jacks a

wise look. 'Being dead is one thing, staying dead is another. You mentioned two of your names but you failed to mention Mister Jacks? I doubt if you can bury him.'

'Right now,' Jacks replied with the greatest sincerity, 'I don't care if the most dangerous thing I ever do again is cross Oxford Street, dodging black cabs in the rain. But you're right, Jacob. Mister Jacks has a will of his own, he can take me over without notice. I learnt today, from reading Catharine's play, just how much a reputation can betray you. I like to think that I am not so predictable as she was but, come the end, everyone knew it was Mister Jacks who was killing them. Catharine was known to favour a long gun and her double shot. Mister Jacks was known for using a .22 and favouring the head shot. I'll need to retire Ivor Johnson. Should I ever resurface, I'll need more than a new identity, I'll need a different gun, a different target to aim at and a whole new style.'

'I'm sure you'll think of someone to become,' Jacob said with a most sincere smile.

'You're never alone with a multiple personality disorder,' Jacks quipped with a grin. 'At least, so they tell me. Whatever, Jacob, it's time I was moving along before I fall asleep on my feet.'

'Where to for now?' Jacob enquired. 'The Savoy?'

'The Savoy is a last resort,' Jacks stated. 'I've got somewhere hopefully more welcoming in mind. The Savoy has great baths but right now I need more than a long soak.'

'It's a long way back to France,' Jacob reminded him.

'But not that far from Belgravia,' Jacks countered.

'Of course,' Jacob responded as realization quickly dawned. 'The bold Miss von Decker.'

'Dear Cassandra,' Jacks corrected. 'Last time we were together she promised that her door would for ever be open to me and right now seems like a good time to learn whether her offer still stands.'

'I'm sure it does,' Jacob said with assurance. 'But before you depart, there's something I feel the need to say.'

Jacks gave Jacob a questioning look.

'We have long had a tacit standing agreement about not talking about what has gone before,' Jacob explained. 'But this time round, circumstances are different. This time round I have been directly involved in your exploits and, having learned what I have, felt what I have, I feel the need to say certain things out loud.'

'Fair enough,' Jacks granted. 'I know the feeling.'

Jacob smiled and looking directly at Jacks, he continued: 'You have never taken the credit for what you have accomplished but, this time, I insist that you do.'

'You do?' Jacks asked with a grin.

'I do,' Jacob confirmed with a small smile.

Jacks smiled back. 'Go on then,' he challenged. 'Convince me I'm a hero, but I bet you can't.'

'Last time round,' Jacob began, 'after the Cassandra affair, I tried to give you the credit for bringing down al-Qaeda's European network but you were having none of it. According to you, the network was brought down by being betrayed by computers and mobile phones—'

'It was,' Jacks claimed.

'Only ultimately,' Jacob qualified. 'And you forget that without your involvement there are no computers or mobile phones to do the betraying. I let the last time go, Billy. But this time round, there is no way you can pass on the credit for what has happened overnight.'

'Try me,' Jacks challenged.

'Let's start with the Snake,' Jacob began. 'What you learnt from him began by bringing down a spy ring that was seriously undermining UK security—'

'I was doing you a service, Jacob,' Jacks reminded him. 'After that, it was you who brought down the spy ring. And, to state a fact, I really don't see anything heroic in torturing a paedophile before killing him and you couldn't convince me otherwise in a thousand years.'

'I would not try,' Jacob stated. 'And you are right, you were doing a service for me, but you stopped doing a service for me the minute you brought me the information I needed.

From then on, all you have done you have done in your own name.'

'Actually,' Jacks corrected him, 'all I did next, I did in the name of the children.'

'I know you did, 'Jacob granted. 'And you have served them well and to a far greater extent than you know.'

'I have?' Jacks questioned.

'Indisputably,' Jacob claimed. 'You began by rescuing a kidnap victim called Jasmin Sek and then you went on to rescue two little boys and two little girls one of whom was Anna, the one you had actually seen and heard being abused.'

'You forgot to mention that, along the way, I did not so much as *kill* two men and a woman, I executed them,' Jacks responded. 'I shot the men from behind and I blew the woman's head to bits. Come on, Jacob, what kind of hero carries on like that?'

'The kind that you are,' Jacob replied. 'Because your part does not end there.'

'It doesn't?'

'It most certainly does not,' Jacob stressed. 'The information you supplied meant that we reached the Wimbledon location before anyone there learned what had happened at Rosewood House. While we were there, three little girls and a little boy were rescued.'

'I'm really glad to hear this,' Jacks said sincerely. 'But it was you and your people who rescued the kids. Without me, you might have got there a bit later but, beginning with Rosewood House, you'd have got everywhere you claim I led you to; you would have rescued the kids, whatever.'

Jacob smiled wanly and shook his head at the man seated before him. 'And there is more, much more,' he said. 'And this is where the machines play their part. The computers taken on the raids have led to the exposure of three worldwide paedophile rings. Web addresses, codes, passwords, everything. The information was passed on and, as we speak, the websites are being investigated by Scotland Yard's paedophile squad and by the FBI equivalent. As with others in the past, these investigations will lead to bank accounts and names and will no doubt lead to many arrests around the globe. It will also undoubtedly mean that many children are rescued from the terrible life they are enduring. Who can say how many? Tens? Hundreds? But whatever the number, they will all begin by owing their freedom to you.'

'The way you just told it,' Jacks countered, 'they owe their freedom to a computer with no sense of loyalty but I'm still very glad to hear the news.'

Once again, Jacob shook his head. 'One last try,' he ventured. 'You cannot deny that you rescued Jasmin Sek or that you delivered her home safely to her father. That alone qualifies as a heroic act.'

Jacks smiled all over his face. 'As I told Jasmin, it's not who rescues you first who counts, it's who rescues you last.'

Another shake of the head from Jacob. 'How did she respond?'

'At first she didn't believe me,' Jacks answered. 'But I convinced her otherwise.'

'I'd wager that you didn't,' Jacob responded. 'Whatever you said to her will not have influenced her thoughts on you. From where I am sitting, you will be her hero all her life.'

'Oh, well,' Jacks said in acceptance as he got to his feet and offered Jacob his right hand. 'As I once said to Cassandra, I've been called worse things than a hero. You can't win them all and who am I to argue with the wise Jasmin?'

As they shook hands, Jacob covered their clasp with his left hand and turned the ceremony into a warm-hearted handshake. 'You are the most interesting of men, Billy.'

'It's merely part of my condition,' Jacks came back with a grin as he broke the handshake. 'But now I have to get moving. I just hope dear Cassandra, assuming she's even at home, is not too disappointed when I fall asleep for a week.'

'I'm sure she'll be happy to watch over you,' Jacob judged. 'Stay in touch.'

'I will,' Jacks said. He turned away and made for the door. He had just reached it when an antique French clock on a mantelpiece chimed out one o'clock. Somewhat disbelievingly, he checked his Omega. When it confirmed that that was indeed the time, a spreading smile lit his weary face. He turned to look at Jacob and said, 'It's one o'clock, Jacob. I kicked off yesterday at noon which means I've been running for twenty-four hours plus. Jack Bauer, eat your heart out.'

And then, with a chuckle, he was gone.

CHAPTER EIGHTEEN

Cassandra von Decker once said to Jacks that life would not be the same without him. Since their parting in Luxembourg, over the weeks of somewhat empty days, she had learned just how prophetic her words had been.

Life truly was not the same.

Cassandra was not entirely certain what it was she so missed about Billy Jacks. She knew the terribly exciting danger they had shared could not possibly be a permanent feature in any relationship they might have but, as she felt excited by just being in his company, she would be happy to see him live a life without danger. The danger had only been a part of their relationship. After that there had been their shared laughter, their sharing of experience but, more than all the rest put together, there had been the way he had treated her.

No one from yesterday and no one from today treated her in any way in the manner that Billy did. At present she was surrounded by sycophants who were over-impressed with her wealth and position. She smiled in remembering how under-impressed Billy had been on learning about her social position. Her money and her possessions made no impression on Billy but she *had* impressed him with her bravery in the face of armed assassins.

What chance did another man have, what chance could she give one, when he would be competing against a man who had once stood her on a toilet seat in a public convenience, put a .45 automatic in her hand, then told her to shoot anyone but him coming through the door?

What chance indeed?

No doubt about it, the man she knew as Billy Jacks was a hard act to follow, and she knew, as she sat there in the splendid living room of her five-million-pound house that if Billy did not turn up before Christmas she would be a woman condemned to live out a lonely life, forever hoping that the next knock at the door would herald the arrival of the man she loved.

Where was Billy right now? Was he still in France, wrapped in the arms of the siren Gabriella? Was he being chased by al-Hashashin? Were they right now trying to kill him? Had he forgotten all about her? Was she just another encounter in his ongoing exciting life? Had he lost her phone number? Her address? Or perhaps forgotten them?

As Cassandra's fears, doubts and hopes careered around her head, she found comfort in the belief that the man she knew and loved as Billy Jacks was an honourable man and if he said that he would come to see her before Christmas then, assuming that no one had killed him in the meantime, that was what he would do.

It was just that the waiting grew harder to bear by the day. On first parting from Billy, she had had much to occupy her mind in regards to dismantling Decker Industries but, over the days, the endless weeks, as one task after another was completed, her mind had come more on more to dwell on whether Billy would turn up today. Every day closer to Christmas, every day without him putting in an appearance made the following day harder to endure.

For fear that he might call when she was out, she had not left the house since arrival. She could not hear the phone ring or someone at the front door without praying that this time it was him, and every time that it was not, she died a little. Like many before her, Cassandra had discovered that love could be destructive as well as creative. Not that her hard-earned knowledge helped her in any way, she still sat up hopefully when the telephone rang, she still listened expectantly when she heard someone at the front door and she still died a little when her hopes were never realized.

Surely Billy would turn up before Christmas.

Surely he would.

Jacks drove away from the Norwood house a tired but an essentially contented man; a day that had begun with a nightmare was ending on a happy note. The little girl Anna was now in good hands and it was looking as though she would be reunited with her mother. If all went well the other rescued children would at least end up with people who loved them and who would take care of them until the day came when they were able to take care of themselves.

Simply because he could never imagine himself in the role, it was easy for Jacks to deny being the hero, but he did know that, without his involvement in the event, little Anna and the other children would still be enduring a life of perpetual abuse. He felt good knowing that he had brought about their eventual freedom.

And seeing Jasmin reunited with her father was a sight that would live with him for as long as he lived. All in all, this had been the most rewarding of all the favours he had done for Jacob. Not only had he been responsible for saving the kids, he had disposed of the mafia assassin, Catharine, a woman who had long had it coming to her, a woman who had been intent on killing him.

The way things had come out, Rasputin was going to be stuck with the problem of his disappearing assassin. By now, Catharine's body and her Mercedes would have vanished off the face of the earth, and though Jacks did not know where Rasputin thought Catharine was, he did know that she was not there.

Jacks appreciated how wonderfully ironic it was that before he'd killed Catharine she had done him the biggest favour of his life by killing a man she thought was him. In doing so she had left al-Hashashin with the problem of *their* missing man. By now, like Catharine and her Merc, he and his BMW would have disappeared from sight and al-Hashashin would never be able to figure out exactly what had happened to him. Not that Jacks was concerned about the questions he had left behind. What mattered was that Rasputin believed Catharine had killed Mister Jacks and that al-Hashashin then believed Rasputin.

Mister Jacks was dead, long live Mister Jacks.

From reflecting on what had gone before, Jacks turned his mind to what might lie ahead. Belgravia was not too far away and, as he drove through the busy afternoon traffic, he wondered what he might find when he got there, while feeling pretty confident that he would find Cassandra waiting with open arms.

After all he had been through, there was no way Fate would end it all by dealing him a bad hand. He had been there that day in the Luxembourg bank when she had sworn her undying love for him. He had seen her face, heard her tone and he was sure that she would be as sincere now as she had been then.

Jacks still did not know what Cassandra meant exactly when she said that she loved him, but he was pretty sure that she did. The way he was feeling right now, a bit of tender, loving care was just what he needed and if he found the Belgravia flat empty he would end the day a very disappointed man. He had just been granted a brand-new life and, for now, at least, he wanted someone to share it with and he wanted that someone to be Cassandra von Decker. How could he ever forget her and her .45 automatic?

With such thoughts, Jacks drove into Belgravia, found Cassandra's address, then went in search of a parking place. Round the first corner he turned, up ahead, a 4 x 4 pulled out from the kerb. As he slid the Ford into the place it left empty, he sensed that he was following the right path and that the Fates were on his side. The chances of finding a convenient, empty parking place anywhere in the borough of Belgravia had to be running at least at 1000:1.

Jacks had made the drive with the windows down and as he got out of the car into the cold afternoon air, sparked by the anticipation of what might follow, his tiredness gave way to hyperactivity as his system boosted his sugar flow until he was running on pure adrenaline.

The easy way would have been for Jacks to cover his back by phoning ahead, but that would not only have been a somewhat cowardly approach, to have done so would have ruled out any drama on the doorstep. If you truly want to learn whether you are welcome somewhere, then turn up there unexpectedly, unannounced and with a suitcase in hand.

When at last he got to ringing Cassandra's front doorbell, Jacks felt as excited as a little boy opening his big present on Christmas morning.

Had Santa brought what he had asked for, or had he not?

When Cassandra heard the front doorbell ring, she instinctively sat up straighter in her chair. The living room door had been left slightly ajar and when she heard, Alice, her middle-aged housekeeper, answer the summons followed by a muffled exchange of voices she expected next to hear the front door being reclosed. When she heard instead the sounds of Alice hurrying up the stairs, hope made her spring to her feet. She was standing expectantly when Alice hurried into the room and announced, in a somewhat excited, breathless voice, that she had a visitor. 'He says to tell you that there's a starving rascal at your door and that he is in need of sanctuary. Is he the one you have been waiting for?'

'Oh, yes,' Cassandra sighed as her whole being was swamped by a pleasure the like of which she had never before endured. 'Did you let him in?'

'I offered,' Alice replied. 'But he said he would wait where he was.'

Of course he did, Cassandra thought as she hurried from the living room and as good as ran down the stairs, Billy would only cross her threshold on an invitation from herself.

When Cassandra reached the front door, she swung it wide open and then stood a moment looking at the man who was the possessor of her heart. He looked back and when she saw his drawn, unshaven face, his red-rimmed eyes with their dilated pupils her concern flew out to him. 'Oh, Billy,' she sighed. 'What have they done to you?' She took him by an arm and led him into the house. 'You look terrible.'

How Jacks smiled. 'Thanks,' he said drily. 'Just be glad you can't see me from the inside.' Holdall in one hand, he let Cassandra lead him up a flight of richly carpeted stairs. 'And it's not so much what they did to me as what I did to them.'

Having prepared for this moment for so long, on reaching the top of the stairs Cassandra led Jacks directly to a door at the end of a corridor. 'This is yours,' she said. She opened the door to reveal a sunlit room furnished with a freshly made, low double bed, bedside table and an armchair, which were reached by crossing a carpet so thick that Jacks thought it needed mowing rather than Hoovering. 'The shower-room is through that door; everything you might need is there.'

As Jacks took it all in he noticed a white towelling robe and a pair of pyjamas laid out on the bed. 'Pyjamas?' he questioned. 'Who's the original owner?'

'You are,' Cassandra replied with a smile. 'Everything you see was obtained with you in mind. I suspected that you never wore pyjamas,' she went on with a teasing grin. 'But as I had no proof either way, I thought I had best be prepared.'

'I wonder where you learned that one?' Jacks asked, smiling as he laid his holdall aside and went through the ritual homecoming ceremony of emptying his pockets.

'Oh, from a man I know,' Cassandra responded as she watched Jacks lay a mobile on the bedside table. The mobile was followed by a wad of banknotes, some loose change, three used cartridges, five live rounds and his Ivor Johnson, which Cassandra smiled to see. 'I wondered whether your friend was with you,' she said.

'I'm going to have to retire him. In his own way he's become a threat to me,' Jacks responded as he took the handkerchief bequeathed by Jasmin from a pocket, folded it neatly and laid it beside the Ivor Johnson.

On seeing the flowery, dainty article, Cassandra's eyebrows rose. 'Can I ask?' she questioned.

Jacks looked directly into Cassandra's emerald eyes, and replied: 'A little girl called Jasmin lent it to me to dry my tears with. Then she said I could keep it if I liked. As trophies go, it stands unique.'

'You cried?' Cassandra said with a hint of astonishment.

'I did indeed,' Jacks confessed as Cassandra took his coat from him and hung it in a wardrobe. 'What I've experienced overnight would have brought tears to a stone.'

'Will you tell me about it?' Cassandra asked.

'I probably will,' Jacks answered. He sat on the bed and took off his boots. 'You prepared all this for me?' he asked, gesturing round the room with an arm. 'I'm touched. And you're right, I never wear pyjamas.' He stood and slid his polo neck sweater over his head to reveal a black T-shirt underneath. 'What about you?' he asked as he approached her and gently gripped her left upper arm.

Cassandra almost blushed. 'I like to wear a nightie,' she replied softly as his touch sent shivers up her back.

'I bet you look a picture,' Jacks said as he leant forward

and kissed her, first on a cheek end then briefly on the lips which invitingly parted at his touch. 'You're a sweetheart, Cassandra, no doubt about it, but I'm just that bit *too* tired. I'll look forward perhaps to seeing you in your nightie but right now I need to sleep. But first, I need to shower, there are smells about me that I don't want to take to bed, particularly a bed so carefully prepared for my comfort.'

With Jacks still holding her arm, Cassandra moved in closer and kissed *him* first on a cheek and then on the lips, the difference being in that her kiss to the lips lasted longer while promising more than his had. 'You smell all right to me, but go and have your shower,' she said softly as he released his hold on her and she released her hold on him.

'All I have to do now,' Jacks said with a small smile that spoke big, 'is stay on my feet a few minutes longer. Close the curtains but switch on the lamp. I don't want to find myself waking up in a strange, dark room.'

When Jacks had disappeared into the shower-room, Cassandra did as he requested. As she did so, she wondered if this meant that the intrepid Mister Jacks carried an inherent fear of the dark. In letting her know about any such fear, in letting her know that he had shed tears, he was trusting her with intimacies that she could not imagine him sharing with many, if with anyone at all.

Cassandra was touched by Billy's apparent trust but she

went downstairs a woman more thrilled by his so obvious show of affection, particularly in the way he had reacted when she kissed him on the lips. He wanted her as a woman, she knew this for certain and, if she was what he wanted, he could have her. He could have her once, twice, a thousand times, he could have her all his life. The man she had parted from in Luxembourg and the man who had just turned up on her doorstep were one and the same. The man she had loved then was the same man as she loved now. How happy such a realization made her.

How terrible it would have been had he turned up at the door a man different from the one she remembered.

Cassandra recalled that Billy liked strong black coffee. She went into the kitchen and switched on the percolator. Alice, who had discreetly vanished on Billy's arrival, offered to make the drinks but Cassandra reserved the pleasure all for herself, taking great care as she collected a tray, two mugs, sugar bowl and a small jug of milk for herself, smiling as she laid two silver teaspoons side by side.

When the coffee was made Cassandra put the pot on the tray and then, much to Alice's disapproval, carried the ensemble upstairs. She was a woman so happy she thought she might cry.

When Cassandra reached Billy's room she was not at all surprised to find him already in bed and fast asleep. She had thought this might happen, had even hoped a little. Billy being asleep meant that nothing needed to be said and that she could just sit by his bedside, drinking coffee, watching over him as she had imagined doing so often.

Although Billy himself did not know it, he badly needed to be taken care of. As Cassandra settled into the bedside chair, coffee in hand, she resolved that she would take care of him for the rest of her life.

Cassandra was under no illusion that Billy could settle down to a life of domesticity, nor would she want him to. Billy had needs no woman could cater for and she believed that the day would dawn when he would move on into some dangerous situation or other. She was already prepared for such an event, her hope being that, though he left her, still he would come back to her because he felt the need of her.

Or perhaps even the desire for her.

EPILOGUE

When Rasputin's people removed Leanna's body from the flat in the Elephant and Castle, as suggested by Catharine, the place was electronically swept and a collection of listening devices was discovered. Such a discovery caused Rasputin concern and a certain amount of puzzlement.

Beginning with the CIA, Mossad and MI5, Catharine was on so many people's wanted lists that it was hard for him to pin down exactly who had been listening in and even harder for him to fathom what the purpose of the exercise had been.

According to Catharine, because of Leanna's indiscretions she had been findable for months. There was no way to tell how long the Elephant and Castle flat had been bugged but, having located Catharine, the people who had planted the bugs had since had ample opportunity to kill her. For some reason they had not, and if they had not, then they had tracked her down for a reason other than to kill her. The only other reason would be to gather information.

As they already knew enough about Catharine they had to be seeking information of a different kind.

Catharine's enemies were Rasputin's enemies. After much thought, he reasoned that someone had been listening in to Catharine with the intention of learning all they could and in the hope that she would lead them to him. Having arrived at such a conclusion he decided to change location for a while.

He had perhaps been too long in Amsterdam.

Catharine had much to answer for but first he would need to find her. Last time they spoke, she claimed to be on her way to Heathrow. He knew the identity she was travelling under but on that day no one of that name flew out of Heathrow or any other major UK airport, which suggested that she had driven into Europe and was now on the run from him.

Catharine had been on the run from someone most of her life. She was trained to disappear and then to blend, she had the funds and the papers that would take her anywhere in the world. Finding her would be difficult but find her he would. She had left a mess behind and he did not like mess.

Catharine was ending her career on a sour note but there was no doubt that she had served him well over the years and she *had* succeeded in killing Mister Jacks, the man who had brought down the greater part of his European spy network and cost him a hundred million dollars.

Al-Qaeda was delighted with the news that Jacks was dead but whereas Rasputin had thought to ask them for payment of a different kind, in order to cover his losses he had been reduced to asking them merely for money rather than change a city scape by a violent explosion.

It was business as usual, and he had a spy-ring to rebuild.

At first Siff and al-Qaeda were delighted to hear of the demise of Mister Jacks, but they were left with the question of what had happened to their man, Mithka, who had not been seen or heard from since leaving the Muswell Hill safe house.

Mithka had left there intent on killing Mister Jacks, so what had happened to him since then?

Catharine was still alive. According to Rasputin, she had killed Mister Jacks; had she also killed Mithka? Or had Mithka killed Mister Jacks and then Catharine killed Mithka? Or had Mithka perhaps been killed in a traffic accident, run over by a London bus? Or had he merely deserted in the face of the enemy?

That was so often the problem with the business they were in: it was so secret that unanswered questions tended to stay unanswered.

Not that the answer really mattered; what mattered was that the hated Mister Jacks no longer walked in the land of the living. It was a pity that Catharine was now reaping the glory instead of Mithka but at least the object of the exercise had been achieved.

The news of Mister Jacks's death had spread around the globe. Jacks's manipulator, the spymaster Jacob, had naturally issued a denial. He was claiming that Jacks had killed Catharine, a claim disproved by the fact that Rasputin must have spoken to Catharine after the event and knew she was alive.

And if Catharine was alive, then Mister Jacks was not.

It was not quite the ending that al-Qaeda had aimed for but it was an ending good enough.

All that really mattered was that Mister Jacks was dead. Allah be praised.

Three days after the event, Jacob arranged for Mithka's body to be burned in a privately owned crematorium in Kent.

The name on the issued death certificate read William John Cranston.

A somewhat ironic ending for Mithka, a man who had set out to make a name for himself.

Two months after the event a young couple, hoping to buy

a run-down property they could work on, were taken by an estate agent to view a rather dilapidated house in Stockwell, south London.

When they arrived, the smell emanating from next door's back garden had the trio gagging. The estate agent, holding a handkerchief to his mouth, looked over the partition fence and saw a large rat rummaging in a ripped refuse bag. He thereupon abandoned any hope of a sale and got in touch with the borough council, who sent a team of exterminators to investigate.

On receiving no answer to their knocking, wearing overalls, rubber boots and surgical masks, the team broke into the house where they discovered the maggot-ridden body of a man which had almost been stripped to the bone by the army of rats that had invaded the house.

Since the event, no one had spared the Snake a thought.